THE OUTLAWS

Unless you've had to draw your guns against the Norcross Brothers, you don't know what trouble means ... Killer bandits both, one was pure evil, while the other went along for the ride.

They'd robbed their boss and left their best buddies to die, naked in the desert, while they headed for Mexico with $90,000 in stolen gold. But each one planned to be the only one to get to Mexico alive.

THE OUTLAWS

Unless you've had to draw your guns against Norcross Brothers, you don't know what trouble m ... Killer bandits both, one was pure evil, while other went along for the ride.

They'd robbed their boss and left their best budd die, naked in the desert, while they headed for M with $90,000 in stolen gold. But each one planned the only one to get to Mexico alive.

THE OUTLAWS

Dean Owen

First published 1973
by Universal Award House Inc

This hardback edition 1992
by Chivers Press
by arrangement with
the author

ISBN 0 7451 4527 2

Copyright © 1973 by Universal-Award House, Inc.
All rights reserved

British Library Cataloguing in Publication Data available

Printed and bound in Great Britain by
Redwood Press Limited, Melksham, Wiltshire

Chapter 1

It was the last day of the long push to Kansas. Jim Norcross eagerly rose in the saddle and pointed at a far-off hint of smoke on the horizon.

"Hey, Ford!" Jim shouted to his older brother. "There she is! Abilene!"

Ford, mounted on a Texas paint, drew abreast of Jim, who was riding at full swing. "Hell, kid, what you so excited about? That's a flyspeck compared to San Antone."

"I bet the smoke is from the steam engines that'll haul our cows east."

"Not *our* cows. We ain't got ten cents in this damn herd." Ford's broad face was flushed.

Jim eyed his brother impatiently and sniffed the dusty air filled with the odors of steer and horse sweat and the rank smell of their own unwashed bodies. Ford had been harping on this theme since they left Texas. Jim also noticed the smell of whiskey on Ford's breath. "You better watch it, Ford," he said.

Ford ignored him. "Hey, little brother, you ready to do the town with ol' Ford?" He grinned, heavy forearms folded on the saddle horn, as he gazed through the dust in the direction of the distant rail head.

Jim persisted, "You know better'n to sneak whiskey. The foreman said he'd fire anyone caught drinking before we got the herd to Abilene."

"Let him fire me." Ford spat into a clump of buffalo grass. "Harper ain't here, anyhow. He done rode on in to locate the commission man."

Jim stood again in the stirrups, brown eyes sweeping the herd that was strung out now. Most of the cattle wore the Killebrew 77 brand, and the rest were from shirt-tail ranches neighboring the big Killebrew spread. Such pooled herds were common wherever there were a number of small ranches close together. Arne Killebrew had not accompanied the herd north because of political upheavals in Austin that he had to handle personally. His foreman, Cale Harper, was boss of the herd. Sure enough, Jim found no sign of him.

He settled back in the saddle, automatically checking the rifle in the boot. Before starting out on the long trail, the regular Killebrew hands had been presented with new Winchesters. Ford had commented that they'd probably damn well earn the weapons before the drive was finished.

Although it was late in the year and the pool herd would probably be the last one up from Texas before the snows hit, Jim was sweating. He took off his hat and wiped his forehead: "I sure look forward to a long soak in a barber's tub," he said.

"Kid, a bath is the last thing you want. Though I admit a man's got to get himself smellin' sweet for the gals." Ford laughed and whacked his knee with a calloused palm, raising a cloud of dust.

Jim saw a cow break suddenly from the herd. Ford made no move to help as Jim, rope end swinging, drove the animal back.

"Why bust your britches?" Ford said when Jim rode up. "What's one cow more or less to Arne Killebrew?"

"He's paying us good enough. We ought to give him a day's work."

"Why you so fond of old man Killebrew all of a sudden?" Ford demanded suspiciously. "You act like he's kinfolks."

He will be, in a way, Jim almost said. Thinking about the Killebrews made his heart pound.

Ford said, "I'll take you to Annie's place, kid. Best house in Abilene, so I hear."

"I told you before we left home to quit calling me kid."

Ford laughed at his twenty-year old brother. "You are a kid till you get your first woman."

"How do you know so damn much?" Jim's face was flaming. He took off his hat again and swung it furiously at the persistent horseflies. "I'm not going with you," he said as he settled his hat low on his forehead.

Ford flung both hands in the air in a mocking gesture. "Lordy, I do declare I seen a halo when you took off your hat."

"Shut up, Ford. Damn it, can't you ever quit riding me?" In other years such an outburst would have been countered by Ford with a backhand to the mouth. But with Jim filling out, older now, Ford either didn't care to test Jim's strength or had grown tired of the game.

"I'm just tryin' to make a man of you, for Chrissake!" Ford was disgusted with Jim's consistent refusal to join him in his prowl of trail town back rooms.

"I'm man enough for myself," said Jim stubbornly.

"And man enough for . . ." He broke off, almost mentioning Nadine Killebrew, the red-haired daughter of their wealthy employer.

Ford said, suddenly curiously, "Man enough for who, kid?"

Jim didn't have to answer, for just then the chuck wagon, driven by Doc Thorne, lumbered by. Thorne grinned, showing a gold tooth. "The Norcross brothers glarin' at each other again," the old man joked. "A bobcat and a Texas mule would get along better'n you two." With the grin still on his weathered face, Thorne drove on ahead. He was a small rancher with a share of the herd who had come along as cook.

Thorne kept the team at a walk so as not to disturb the herd by any unusual sounds, such as the clatter of pots and pans in the chuck wagon. They had come all these miles without a stampede and Jim was hopeful that with the drive almost over nothing would happen. The return home couldn't be too soon for him. His throat dried as he thought of Nadine's huge green eyes and the excitement of her lips.

"One of these days I'll rub that grin off Doc's face with a bootheel," Ford grumbled. He dug a flask from under his shirt, took a drink and held it out to his brother.

Jim shook his head. "Not me. Harper could come back from town any time."

"Mebby he rode off with the herd money." Ford took another drink, then stowed the flask. "Jeez, with that much money I'd buy out Annie's place an' let you stay for a year."

"Let's get one thing straight, damn it. I don't want your kind of life. I've told you often enough!"

"Aw, you act like a man in love."

"I am."

Ford gave a whoop of surprise. "You ain't kidding,

are you? Who you in love with?"

"Forget it."

"I bet it's that old maid school teacher where you got all your fancy book learnin'."

"Cut it out, Ford. You just might be surprised when we get back to Texas."

"Oh yeah? What kind of surprise, little brother?" Ford narrowed his hazel eyes, bloodshot from dust and frontier whiskey.

Jim drew a breath and decided to let out his secret in the hope that his brother would leave him alone. "When I get back home, I figure to marry Nadine Killebrew."

"The boss's daughter? You mean . . ." Ford pulled his horse to a halt, surprised for a moment. Then he threw back his head and gave a howl of laughter. A big steer swung about, tips of its wicked horns dangerously close to Ford's mount. Jim, sensing possible disaster, rode between Ford's horse and the red steer and drove it away with his rope.

Jim coiled his rope and said angrily to Ford who was still laughing, "Quiet down. You trying to set those cows to running?"

Ford wiped his eyes. "You marry Nadine Killebrew?"

"I aim to," Jim said stiffly.

"She *say* she'd marry you?"

"We got an understanding."

"Oh sure, an understanding," Ford scoffed.

"I'm buying her a ring in Abilene."

"You're loco, kid. Hell, Nadine is so stuckup rich you couldn't even walk in her dust."

"Sure. That's why she gave me this." Jim pulled a daguerreotype from his shirt pocket with shaking hands. He brushed stirrups with Ford and shoved the small photo into Ford's hands. It showed a smiling

Nadine in a traveling suit at the fancy school she attended in Baton Rouge.

Ford reined in to stare at the photo with its graceful inscription: "To the most wonderful boy at 77 ranch."

Ford laughed again, not as boisterously as before. He returned the photograph to his brother, saying, "Kid, she's handed out them daguerres..."

"Shut up, Ford. You're always tearing down things you don't know nothing about. Just keep your mouth shut about Nadine."

Ford shook his head knowingly and jerked his hat brim low as he faced into the sun. He beckoned to one of the other hands. "Hey, Bascom! Bascom Trent!"

Trent, a large man in his late twenties, had worked at the 77 ranch for over a year. A lot of people wondered how a native Texan who had enlisted in the Union Army had ever come to work for a diehard Reb sympathizer like Arne Killebrew. In fact, Jim recalled, Harper had been riding Trent about the War all the way up the trail.

Trent swung his horse over their way and said in his gravelly voice, "Ford, you got any more of that whiskey?"

"Sure. But first tell me. You got that daguerre you was showin' me last month?"

"The one of the Killebrew filly? Yeah..."

Jim rode between his brother and the bulky Trent so that both men had to rein aside. "Don't call her that again, Trent!" Jim said coldly. "I mean it!"

Trent stared at him, a red flush slowly creeping along his high cheekbones. "Who the hell you talkin' to like that?"

"Show Jim the picture," Ford urged. "Do it an' I'll give you a jolt of Kansas lightning." Ford pulled the flask from his shirt.

Eyeing the whiskey, Trent fished in a pocket for the

daguerreotype and handed it to Jim Norcross. Jim stared. It was the same pose—Nadine smiling at the camera of the itinerant photographer who took pictures of the girls at the private school. Stunned, Jim stared at the same words that had been written across the face of the photograph Nadine had given him.

Jim brushed the daguerreotype aside. "It's not the same writing," he said angrily.

Trent returned it to his pocket. "Mebby her hand was a little shaky the night she give it to me." He winked at the grinning Ford. "The moon was sure bright that night an' she was sweet as honeysuckle ... out by Number Two windmill ..."

Jim leaned over in the saddle and swung hard with his right. He caught Trent squarely on the cheekbone. Trent made a grab for the saddle horn, lost his grip and fell backwards into a pile of buffalo droppings not more than a day old. He came to his elbows, swearing. Cattle veered, streaming around the fallen cowhand, some of them snorting and rolling their eyes at the strange figure of unhorsed man. Oblivious of the milling cattle, Trent made a grab for his gun.

Ford shouted, "Touch that gun an' you're dead!"

"Keep outa this, Ford!" Trent yelled, but he paused, catching a glimpse of the tight face of the older Norcross brother. His hand fell away from his gun. He got slowly to his feet and rubbed at the swelling on his cheek. "What the hell· ails your loco brother?" he demanded of Ford.

Jim's horse had buck-jumped a few yards, but Jim rode it back and handed the reins to Ford. He stepped down, unbuckled his gun belt and hung it over the saddle horn.

"Trent," Jim said to the big Texan, "I aim to teach you some manners."

Trent had started to pick up his fallen hat and

brush himself off when he realized that he had landed on the buffalo droppings. With a snarl of disgust he tossed his hat aside and lunged at Jim. Jim waited, feet planted wide, fists clenched. Trent's fist swung with such force that had it landed Jim's face would have been smashed. Jim ducked the roundhouse, taking it on the shoulder. But the power of the blow rocked him. He swung a left that caught Trent under the heart. Trent grunted in pain and rage and let fly a flurry of blows, some of which connected with Jim's jaw and rib cage. A little dazed, Jim managed to power a right into Trent's solar plexus. The paunchy cowhand doubled up with a gasp, and as he was straightening up, Jim smashed him twice in the face. Trent fell heavily, sprawling full length on the prairie.

Sandy Burkhardt, one of the pool ranchers, spurred up, yelling, "What you hellions trying to do? Spook the herd? Now call it off or I'll bust heads." The lanky, mustached cowman brandished his rifle like a club.

Trent climbed up on his horse, his face bleeding. He glared at Jim Norcross. "We'll finish this later."

"I'll be waiting." Jim was still trembling, with rage over the things Bascom Trent had implied about his girl.

Tom Cass, all jowl and belly, a rep for a rancher who had not made the trip, reined in beside Burkhardt. He glowered at Jim and the departing Bascom Trent. "You stampede this herd after we trailed it all the way from Texas, an' I'll nail your hides to the barn wall." Jim rode off after some straying cattle.

When Burkhardt and Cass learned from Ford the reason for the brawl they shook their heads. "She'll be the death of some young fella yet," said Burkhardt, then heeled his horse after the herd that was beginning to spread out along the Kansas flatlands. It took an hour to bunch them again.

When they had a chance to draw an easy breath, Jim rubbed the knuckles of his right hand which had connected so savagely with Trent's hard face. He felt a swelling along his side where his ribs were bruised.

Ford, watching him, laughed. "I always knew you'd be a tough one if you ever got fired up enough to show your fangs."

"He had no right saying those things about Nadine."

"You better keep your eye open for that Bascom Trent," Ford warned.

"I'll watch out. Don't worry none about that."

Ford let his breath out in a long sigh. "For ten cents worth of Yankee paper money I'd never go back to Texas." He glanced at Jim. "If you had a lick of sense, you wouldn't go back either."

"Well, I aim to," Jim said.

"That Killebrew gal ain't worth it, Jim. No woman is."

"How would you know—the kind of woman you go around with?" Far ahead Jim could see a string of cattle cars inching along the horizon, pulled by a smoke-belching engine.

Ford's dark brows were lifted in surprise. "You really courtin' the Killebrew gal, huh?"

Jim nodded, not wishing to discuss it, but Ford pushed on. "Then how come Bascom Trent's got her picture same as you?"

"Likely he stole it."

"How about the writin' she put on it?"

"It's not the same as on mine," Jim replied stubbornly. Jim tried to tell himself that it was a forgery, that Trent had either done the writing himself, trying to make it look as if written by a girl, or had gotten some fancy woman in Saddleback to do it for him.

They were riding again at full swing, with the extra hands hired on for the drive spread out at various points around the herd of three thousand head. Ford said, "Listen, kid, I want to tell you somethin' about women. Nadine Killebrew, she's uppity an' she . . ."

"Look, Ford," Jim said, turning in the saddle so quickly that he felt a twinge of pain across his bruised ribs, "you want some of the same I gave Trent, I'll give it to you."

"All right, all right. Take it easy. You used to be easy goin'. Now you got a trigger temper. What ails you, anyhow?"

Jim relaxed a little. "It's just we don't think alike, Ford. I'm thinking about the future. And a wife's a lot of responsibility for a man to take on."

Ford's brown, sweat-streaked face seemed thoughtful. "Responsibility, eh? Wouldn't be so tough with the Killebrew money. If you could get your hands on it, that is." He scowled as they rode along the broad trail left by the many herds that had passed over this hardpan on the way to the Kansas rail head.

"We won't need any of old man Killebrew's money," Jim said. "I got me over two hundred dollars saved up. I aim to buy some land over west of Saddleback."

"You *are* loco."

"Settle down is what I aim to do, Ford. Have a place of my own and kids to pass it on to."

"That ain't the life for me. An' you'll get tired of it quick enough too."

Jim shook his head impatiently.

"But then if you was married to that gal, Killebrew would likely set you up real good . . ." Ford said with a grin.

Jim rode on ahead before he lost his temper. Before he went a dozen yards he saw that Billy Coyle, one of the regular 77 hands, was in trouble. The diminutive Coyle was trying to shunt three big steers back into the herd. Two of them lumbered off without a glance at the little bowlegged cowhand wielding a rope. But the third one lunged at Coyle's horse. Before Coyle could be unseated, however, Jim came between them, his rope end swinging to strike the big animal solidly between the eyes. For an instant the steer's red eyes glared at Jim and its feet braced as if to charge, then it wheeled for the herd. Jim urged it along with his stinging rope end. The animal mingled with the others, shaking its immense horned head from side to side.

Coyle grinned at Jim. "Thanks, Jim. It's been a damn long trail an' I reckon I got careless."

Ford spurred up. "You tryin' to kill yourself, little brother?" Ford grinned. "With you dead, that Killebrew money will take wings."

"Will you shut up?" Jim rode away, coiling his rope.

Chapter 2

Later in the day Jim felt his spirits lift as he gazed at the buildings of Abilene dead ahead. As he had told Ford earlier, all he looked forward to was a bath and some sasparilla to rinse out his mouth. Then it would be a fast trip home—just as fast as his roan could carry him. And in his pocket would be the ring to put on Nadine's finger. Before leaving home he had told her that he planned to buy a ring and she had looked at him with her big green eyes and said, "With a diamond big as a riverboat searchlight, I bet." She had patted his cheek. He could still feel the soft palm of her hand against his face. He wondered if Ford had ever been in love with a girl. He thought about asking Ford's advice in buying the ring, Ford having had more experience in trail towns. But he knew Ford would only make fun of him.

As he jogged along, occasionally flicking his rope at a wayward cow, Jim thought of the day they had left Texas. Nadine had ridden out to where the herd was bunched, her braids bouncing at the back of her silk shirt, her teeth flashing in the sunlight. She smiled at him and said, "You be careful on the trail, cowboy." Leaning over in the saddle, she brushed his cheek with her lips.

Now that he thought back on it, Jim recalled one of the cowhands giving a bleat of laughter. Bascom Trent, sure as hell. He remembered seeing Trent turn aside, his big shoulders jerking as he laughed. He wished that he had hit Trent harder today. And if he kept making hints about Nadine. . . . He jerked his .44 free of leather then slowly put it back in the holster.

Ford, riding a few feet to Jim's right, said, "Who you aim to gun for, kid?"

"Maybe you if you don't leave me alone." Jim said it with a tight smile.

"You never been in a tough trail town before, kid. Don't go pullin' a gun like that, or you might get buried there."

"Yeah, I hear you," Jim muttered. He let go of the gun and wiped his sweaty hand on his shirt.

For the remainder of the push to Abilene, Jim daydreamed about Nadine and his coming marriage. Arne Killebrew might be a little grumpy at first because his only child intended to marry a common cowhand. But when Jim explained his plans, and reminded the old man that he himself started out as a cowboy, he knew Killebrew would come around. Jim could almost hear him say, "Good luck, son. If you ever mistreat my gal I'll whup the hide right off your bones." And Jim would grin back at his future father-in-law. Arne Killebrew would stage a big wedding and invite some of his Austin cronies. Jim would hate all the showing off and Nadine would feel the same way. But they'd humor the old man. And when it was over they'd drive out in the second-hand buggy and the guests would throw rice and wish them luck and Nadine in her white gown would blush and blow kisses at her father.

Jim smiled a little ironically at his fantasy. But, hell, if a man didn't have dreams, what was the use of living on this earth? He didn't intend to drink and gamble his life away as Ford was doing, taking pleasure with those women who would greet a man with a smile, then yawn when he was going out the door.

They herded the cattle into one of the big holding grounds near the Kansas-Missouri tracks. As the packing house men took charge of the herd, Cale Harper, the foreman, rode out from town. He was a dark-haired man in his mid-forties, thick through the neck and shoulders. He had worked for the 77 ranch since before the war.

Harper paid off the extra hands first, those hired on just for the trail job. They whooped and hollered their way toward town, anxious to spend their money, which would be gone within twenty-four hours, probably less. Then Jim and the other regular hands and pool ranchers were called to a spot of shade by a railroad shed.

Nine men in all faced Harper. There was Trent, Burkhardt, Doc Thorne, Billy Coyle, Tom Cass, and two other cowhands named Jennings and Reivers. Jim and Ford made up the rest of the group.

Harper was staring at Trent's face. "Chuck wagon run over you?"

Trent flushed. "Before we get back to Texas you'll see a face lookin' worse than mine." He shot an ugly sidelong glance at Jim Norcross.

Harper caught the look and guessed there had been some sort of fracas on the trail in his absence. "Well, it's my opinion that a good Reb can beat a Union man any day of the week," he said, giving Jim a sly grin. Jim shifted uncomfortably. Although he had been too young for the War, some of the older men were still fighting it, so it seemed. He wished Harper would get on with whatever he had to say. At times the foreman could be almighty long-winded.

Harper frowned and added, "But you boys better get any grudges settled before tomorrow morning 'cause our job ain't over yet." He scanned the surprised faces of the regular 77 hands. "The boss gave you boys each a new Winchester. A bonus. Now you'll earn it."

Ford, standing beside Jim, muttered, "I told you we'd get nothin' free from that tight old bastard."

"Shut up, Ford," Jim said under his breath.

"We're not going to make much time on the trip home," Harper said. "It'll take us about as long as it did to get here."

Jim felt his heart drop. He had counted on a swift return trip. Harper rambled on about how much Arne Killebrew counted on the loyalty of his men and his neighbors who made up the pool. Jim noticed something ugly in Ford's expression as he listened to the foreman. When Ford came to work for the Killebrew outfit some months ago Jim thought his brother had changed. Ford had seemed jovial, eager to please after spending a year in jail down at Reeves Point. It hadn't been the first time Ford had been in jail. As far back as Jim could remember, Ford had been in one kind of trouble or another, starting when he was twelve and had stolen a neighbor's horse.

Only Ford's age had saved him from being strung up when they caught him that time. Now Jim was afraid Ford was getting ready to kick over the traces again.

Jim was aware of Harper saying, "Now the reason

for all this is that the boss wants pay for the herd in gold. There was a letter from him waitin' for me in Abilene when I went in today, giving me full instructions."

Sandy Burkhardt licked at a corner of his mustache and laughed. "Everybody knows Arne won't take what he calls Yankee paper money or Yankee bank drafts."

"So as we'll be packin' that gold, it'll take us a while to get back to Texas," Harper explained. "And it'll take all ten of us to guard it."

"The boss gives us new rifles that he likely bought cheap," Ford grunted. "Some pay for what we got to do."

Harper ignored Ford. "There'll be hombres who know we got this money with us. No way we can stop that. But I got a Greener and so has Doc Thorne." With a grin, he gestured at the sawed-off shotgun on his saddle. "Anybody tries for that gold will have their heads fulla buckshot."

"We'll get that gold back to Texas," vowed Sandy Burkhardt.

Harper said, "Now that we got that settled, I might as well give you boys the rest of the news. Might be nice for you to chip in together an' buy a gift for the bride. Harper opened Killebrew's letter and read the postscript: "Good thing I stayed home instead of trailing with you boys. Nadine got married last week to a young fella from Austin, a lawyer. Comes from a fine family..."

Jim heard no more. Nadine's face seemed to rise in front of his eyes as she said with a little smile, "Sure, I'll wait for you, cowboy." It couldn't be true! He was aware of his brother's sharp, derisive eyes on his face.

Bascom Trent shrugged as he gingerly rubbed at one of the purplish swellings on his face. "Seems you an' me busted ourselves up for nothin'. Even so I won't forget it." He stalked over to where the horses were bunched.

With a bad try at a grin Jim said, "Hey, Mr. Harper, you're sure you're not just joshing us?"

"Here it is in black and white." Harper showed him the letter. Jim glanced across the words: "fine family . . . they'll live in Austin . . ." "How about that," he managed to say as he handed the letter back.

"The boss is no fool," said Harper, folding the letter. "Reckon he knew Nadine figured to get married an' that's why he stayed to home. . . . Hey, boy, you okay?"

"Yeah, just dandy," Jim said, rather unconvincingly.

"Don't tell me you was sweet on Nadine Killebrew?" Harper laughed and shook his head. "Every cowhand who ever come to work on the 77 was sweet on her. Cheer up, son. You never had a chance. I could've told you that if you'd asked me."

Harper paid them off. As Jim pocketed the coins glumly, Harper concluded, "Have your fun in town, boys. But be here at nine in the mornin' ready to take that gold back to Texas."

Ford slapped Jim on the back and said, "Let's go, kid."

The Norcross brothers rode in silence toward town. At one of the tracks an engine spotting empty cattle cars on a siding blocked them for a time. Finally, when the tracks had cleared, their horses clattered across the steel rails and Ford cleared his throat.

"Now mebby you'll believe what I say about women."

"She said she'd wait for me," Jim said stubbornly, but even as he spoke he recollected that even when she said it he hadn't been sure she meant it.

"See what a damn fool thing it is to fight over a woman?" Ford pointed out. "Trent would've killed you if I hadn't warned him off. He ain't scared of you, kid."

Jim nodded. Seemed like Ford was right about everything recently. A few cowboys, firing guns in the air, were reeling along one of the side streets.

"You were lucky to get in the first punch with Trent," Ford said. "Next time you mind what your big brother says. Now let's go get some whiskey, then we'll go over an' enjoy the parade at Annie's."

After putting up their horses, the brothers entered the nearest saloon where Ford steered Jim through a jam of cowhands around gaming tables. Jim leaned against the bar at a place where Ford had shoved other men aside to make room for them. Men grumbled but one look at Ford ended any protest.

Jim stared at the glass of whiskey Ford had poured for him. He drank it off in one gulp, somehow managing not to choke. Two women pushed their way to the bar and one of them took Ford's arm, another Jim's. Jim pulled away.

The girl said to Ford, "What's the matter with your friend?"

"He's got a busted heart a mile wide," Ford laughed.

"Is that all?" The girl looked at Jim and said, "I can fix that, cowboy." But Jim turned his back.

Ford waved the women aside and leaned toward Jim. "Best thing that ever happened to you, kid. Now you got your whole life ahead of you, an' no women to worry about. At least not the kind who'll try to rope you down with a passel of kids and 'responsibilities.'" He gave the word a derisive emphasis and Jim remembered with embarrassment what he had said earlier in the day. Ford went on, "No, ain't nothin' counts in this world but them things you takes by usin' your brains."

Jim said nothing.

Ford refilled their glasses and lifted his in a toast. "Here's to us, kid. In *Mayheeco* I'll show you *senoritas* that'll make you forget Nadine Killebrew ever lived."

"Mexico," Jim muttered as he absently slid his glass in wet rings on the bartop. "Who's going to Mexico?"

"Down there I'll show you green grass an' trees an' more water than a cowman could ever wish for."

"You never been in Mexico," said Jim.

"When I was in jail at Reeves Point there was a fella who had done a little rustling off some of them big *hacendados* across the line. Ended up with a good-sized herd. He was a big man in Mexico."

"He must have been right smart to end up in the same jail with you."

"He got in trouble with *politicos*. You an' me, Jim, when *we* get to Mexico we'll corner us off a piece of that good grass..."

"What makes you think I'm going to Mexico?"

Ford shook his head. "You know damn well you can't go back to work for Killebrew. You couldn't stand the sight of that gal comin' home to visit."

"I reckon you're right about that," Jim admitted grudgingly.

After they had some dinner, Jim begged off from joining Ford in a tour of the trail town's parlor houses, saying that he wanted nothing more to do with females, at least for the time being. Ford laughed and sent him off to a hotel with a bottle of whiskey for company.

Jim sat on the edge of the bed staring out the window at the revelry in the street below. Unsteady cowboys and gaudily dressed women spilled out of saloon doors. There were the sounds of an occasional gunshot, a women's laughter and cursing from some cowhand thwarted either in love or in a poker game. In the distance he could see the dark mass of Texas herds faintly visible in the moonlight. Cattle cars banged on sidings and steam engines blew gusts of hot vapor into the night sky.

Jim drank steadily. Along about midnight he managed to fumble Nadine's daguerreotype from his pocket. As he looked at the smiling face his mouth twisted. He flung the picture across the room and hurled the empty bottle after it. With a groan he sank back on the bed and soon fell into a troubled sleep.

At daybreak Ford came into the room, red-eyed but fairly steady on his feet. The sight of the discarded picture and the broken bottle made him chuckle. "You're learnin' fast, kid. Now move over. I need an hour's sleep before we have to go pick up that gold."

"Easy, easy," Jim groaned as Ford sat down heavily in the bed.

"Aw, is your head painin' you a smidge, little brother?" Ford joked.

"Never again . . . never again."

"Just you wait'll we get to *Mayheeco*," Ford said as he rolled over, crowding Jim against the wall.

"What are we gonna do in Mexico?"

"We'll buy up some land and cows and do some ranchin' on our own."

"With what?" Jim asked. "I've only got two hundred dollars saved up and you sure ain't got nothin'."

"We're not going to need your two hundred bucks, sonny boy."

"I must be still drunk or loco or both. What the hell are you talkin' about?"

"Go to sleep, kid. You'll find out ever'thing in good time."

Chapter 3

The next morning was clear and bright and the town was almost as lively as it had been the night before. Jim had no stomach for breakfast, but managed to down a cup of coffee. In the cafe they learned that some of the extra hands who had come north with them were in jail. One of them had been cut up in a knife fight and another had been thrown from a second-floor window during a brawl. Due to his inebriation he had suffered only broken ribs and a sprained ankle.

"If you got money enough," Ford confided to his brother, "you can always buy your way out of jail."

"Maybe you better save up for the next time you're in," Jim said with a grin.

Ford only smiled. "There's other ways of gettin' rich."

During the ride out to camp Jim kept his hat brim low, shading his eyes from the climbing sun. His head felt like there was a dentist's chisel cutting into his skull.

Despite his night of carousing, Ford seemed jovial and even lifted a hand in greeting to Bascom Trent. Trent nodded, glared at Jim, and said, "Did the little boy drink too much white lightning? He looks green around the gills."

"Leave him alone, Bascom," Ford said with a smile. "He's only a kid. Let's us try an' get along. We got a lot of miles to cover all the way back to Texas."

"And we'll have that damned money to guard." Trent grunted and swung in beside Ford's Texas paint. "Wish the old man had taken a bank draft for the cows."

"He says Yankees own all the banks," Ford chuckled. "Can't trust a Yankee, he says."

Trent tensed and twisted his face, still livid from the fight the day before, into a snarl. "An' I reckon you agree with him, eh Ford?" he said belligerently.

"What you so riled about? You're Texan, ain't you?" Ford's eyes were innocent.

"You know damn well I was with Grant."

"Guess I'd forgot."

Cale Harper, coming from another direction, caught up with them in time to hear the last. "One thing I could never figure out," said the foreman, "was why the old man made me hire a native Texan that fought North."

"You keep on tryin' to figure it out," Trent said bluntly, and rode away from them.

Harper muttered under his breath, "turncoat," then turned to stare at Jim. "You look like hell, kid. Did you drink Kansas dry last night?"

"No, sir. Not quite."

"Look, Jim, lemme set one thing straight. From here on out you call me Cale. Forget the sir. You done good on the trail comin' up an' when we get back home I'll see about gettin' you a dollar more a month." His heavy hand rested on Jim's shoulder.

Jim was about to say that he wasn't sure he was going to stay at the Killebrew ranch when he saw Ford's faint shake of the head. Jim said to Harper, "The dollar a month will come in mighty handy."

"You stick with us, Jim," Harper said. "One day you might even make *segundo*."

"Should only take about ten years, ain't that right, Cale?" Ford drawled. Harper, not realizing Ford was joshing him, answered, "Well, not ten. More like seven or eight."

"That's sure something to think about." Jim said.

Harper had turned and was now eying Ford critically. As if viewing his brother through Harper's eyes, Jim noticed the deep lines bracketing Ford's mouth and the pouches under his bloodshot eyes. Jim thought, *Ford is sure old for his age.* He supposed that was what war and jail did to a man. Jim wondered if Nadine's treachery would eventually leave a mark on his own face.

Harper said to Ford, "I'd make you the same kind of offer I made Jim, but I reckon you're a drifter at heart."

"I sure wouldn't want to stick around eight years," Ford drawled turning his head to hide a smile.

The rest of the men came riding up, yawning and scratching. In the distance Jim could see their herd being shunted toward one of the rail sidings where cattle cars were spotted. Three thousand head of beef at around thirty dollars a head. That would add up to a lot of gold.

As if reading his mind Harper turned to them all and said, "Let's go get us some cow money." They rode to a mail car on a siding where some lawmen holding rifles were longing. The big red-haired one introduced himself as Sheriff Little. Harper dismounted and shook hands with him.

A rotund man wearing a hard hat and an ink-black undertaker's suit was standing in the mail car. He spoke to Harper. "We brought your payment in gold, as you requested. Step inside and we'll count it out for you."

Harper climbed into the mail car. There was no one else within a half mile of them, Jim noticed. The men crowded around the open door as the black-suited man and his assistant began bringing out sack after sack of money.

"I been ranchin' for fifteen years," Sandy Burkhardt said with a shake of his head. "I never seen near that much money."

Jim nodded at the stacks of large eight-sided coins now being set out on the table in the mail car. "Never saw money that looked like that," he said.

"Fifty-dollar gold pieces," Burkhardt explained.

Harper smiled down at Jim. "Don't make that extra dollar a month I promised you look like much, does it?"

Jim shook his head. "Gotta start somewhere, though," he commented. Ford caught his eye and gave him an approving wink.

Jim watched Ford as his brother turned away from the group, pretending disinterest in the proceedings. Ford sure had something on his mind, all right, and knowing Ford it was bound to be trouble.

When the money was counted, Ford said, "You ever see so much *dinero* in one place, kid?"

"Sure is a heap of gold," Jim admitted.

The four burros Harper had purchased were brought up to the mail car to be loaded. The coins were scooped into leather sacks which were in turn wrapped in burlap so as to minimize the possibility that someone would think they held money. The sacks were tied to the burro's pack saddles and bedrolls were lashed on top of everything.

When they were ready to pull out, Sheriff Little said, "You fellas sure got a fur piece to go with that money. There's outlaws, renegade Indians, and God knows what else between here and Texas."

"We'll get home with it," Harper assured him.

"We can stand off an army if we got to," Doc Thorne said and pointed to the sawed-off shotgun in a special saddle scabbard.

Trent grumbled, "I oughta have that shotgun 'stead of that old man."

Harper looked at him sharply, then drew him aside. Jim was close enough to overhear the foreman say, "I just want you to know you're the one man I ain't sure of. A man who's been a turncoat once, is just likely to try it again."

"I never was a turncoat."

"I heard different."

"Harper, I've had enough of your dirty cracks. My pa and Arne Killebrew was boys together. Killebrew didn't turn against our family just 'cause we went along with Sam Houston's idea about not bustin' up the Union. Next time you think of calling me a turncoat you consider how you'd like to lose your job, 'cause I can make trouble for you for sure."

Harper eyed the big Texan. "So that's how come the boss hired you on. Why didn't you tell me this before?"

"Figgered it was none of your business," Trent said sullenly.

Harper looked at him with a little more respect, but said, "If I want you to have a shotgun, I'll let you know." He looked toward Doc Thorne. "Doc ain't a young man for that kind of shootin', that's for sure."

He tramped back to where the rest of the men were mounting up, encircling the loaded burros.

The commission man, perspiring in his black suit, gave Harper a paper to sign. "Gold coins minted in California in exchange for Texas cows." The man smiled. "We'll get these cows to the packing house safe and sound. I wish you the same luck with the gold."

Harper swung into the saddle and looked at his men. "Boys, till we get this gold in the Killebrew safe, we keep our eyes open and our powder dry." He led the way across the tracks, the loaded burros stepping daintly over the rails.

Later in the day Ford casually reined in beside Jim who was bringing up the rear. Ford jerked his head, indicating for Jim to drop back. The rest of the party with the burros was some distance ahead when Ford finally spoke.

"Step down an' pretend your hoss has a loose shoe. I'll keep my eye on the rest of the boys."

Jim hesitated, then dismounted and glanced at the party ahead.

"Had to talk where nobody could hear us," Ford said, rolling a cigarette.

"Talk about what?" Jim asked as he pretended to inspect a horseshoe.

"You game to go in with me an' take that money?"

Jim brushed the gravel off the left forefoot of his roan as he tried to figure out how to answer his brother. "I'm not sure I want a posse on my tail the rest of my life," he finally managed.

"Dammit, kid, how do you expect to get anywhere in this world? How d'you think Killebrew got his start?"

"Hard work, I suppose."

"He swung a wide loop, that's how he got his start."

Ford lit his cigarette. "Every cowman in Texas that amounts to a hill of beans done the same thing. Besides, having someone after you doesn't mean you'll get caught."

Jim felt cold sweat trickle down his side. His horse was restless so Jim let his forefoot go and slowly stood up. "A man turns thief," he said, "and he *never* loses the brand." Jim squinted up at Ford silhouetted against the sun and felt the pain in his throbbing skull.

"There's most ninety thousand dollars in them sacks, bucko. That'd be mighty fine to have in them green hills of old *Mayheeco*."

"If we could ever make it across the border."

"Won't be nobody down there bigger than us, kid." Ford suddenly tensed and said, "Here comes Harper."

Jim saw the foreman pounding up, his face red with anger. "What the hell's goin' on?" he demanded.

"Jim said his hoss had a loose shoe," Ford drawled. "I dropped back to give a hand if he needed it."

Harper glared at Jim. "Well, *is* it loose?"

"No sir, he was favoring it and I thought I better have a look."

"Next time sing out," Harper said. "We got to stick close together." The foreman's gaze swung to Ford. "You should know that, Ford, you bein' in the war an' all."

Jim mounted up, wondering just how much Harper actually knew about Ford's past—the year in jail at Reeves Point, the other things Ford had done.

"Won't happen again, Cale," Ford said. He seemed sincere.

The three of them rode to where the rest of the outfit waited at the crest of a long grade. "After this we keep together," Harper counseled. "Anybody got a shoe loose or something, you yell. We'll pull up right there an' wait till it gets fixed. *Comprenden?*"

"Yes, sir," Jim said.

"Now let's get in a few more miles before sundown. And for Christ sake stop sirring me, Jim." Harper grinned at him.

Then he frowned and took Jim aside. "By the way, I may have been a little hasty with my promises earlier today. I didn't know Trent was in so good with the old man. An' he's had a lot of experience." Harper's smile was stiff. "You'll work into a good job anyhow."

"But not as *segundo*," Jim guessed.

"Like I said, Trent's had experience."

Jim shrugged, not really surprised or giving a damn.

Harper misinterpreted his look. "Don't be so downhearted," Harper said. "77 is a big ranch—lots of money for everyone. Or is it Nadine got you down? I been at 77, a long time. She's been bustin' hearts since she was twelve." Harper leaned over in the saddle to give Jim a knuckle in ribs. "Seems like she busted your heart proper, huh?"

"Don't mean nothing to me, Cale."

"That's the way to talk, Jim. She was ten miles in the sky above you. Trent's not letting it hang on *him* like an anvil. And neither are any of the other boys. I know Nadine . . ." Harper's voice was edged with embarrassment. "Well, anyhow, I'm glad she's married now. Best thing for everybody. You ever see the fella she married?"

"Not that I know of."

"He was at the ranch a few times. Big tall fella . . ."

"Yeah, I remember," said Jim. "Dude kind of. Older than her, though."

"She needs an older hand. She'd been engaged to Tom for most a year. Thought she'd never make up her mind. Like I said, best for everybody that she got herself a husband." Harper cleared his throat. "Like as not she'd have got one of you young fellas killed if she hadn't stopped bein' honey sweet to the lot of you."

"Reckon." Jim stared at a sweep of wooded hills ahead.

"One thing about my kid brother," Ford said, giving Jim a meaningful look, "he don't aim to let no female rope him to the home corral. That right, Jim?"

"I don't aim to get married ever."

Ford beamed at him.

The next day fleecy clouds drifting from the north were followed by more sombre looking thunderheads which let loose and showered them for over an hour. Rain pounded hatbrims and slickers and dripped down the cowboys' necks.

Sandy Burkhardt, who had dropped back to ride beside Jim, looked grimly at the pack burros struggling through the mud. "I've knowed Arne Killebrew for quite a spell. An' I've knowed him to do damn fool things in his time. But us ten hombres ridin' herd on all that gold is the worst."

"He should've taken a check," Ford said with a straight face. "Then all we'd have to do is ride home an' look at the scenery on the way."

Burkhardt smiled through his mustache. "You young fellas would likely do more than look at scenery. We pass a lot of towns on the way south."

"Well, we sure can't do no drinkin' or waltzin' the gals now," Ford said. "Watchin' that gold is serious business."

"It sure is," Burkhardt said. "I can't afford to lose a dollar of my share. Mebby Killebrew will give you boys an extra five dollars when you get back."

"Jeez, that'd be mighty fine," Ford said, and Jim,

watching his brother's face, saw that it was all Ford could do to contain his laughter.

"I tell you one thing," confided Burkhardt. "It was mighty smart of Cale to buy them two sawed-off shotguns in Abilene. Any robbers try to jump us an' they'd get cut off at the boottops with them Greeners."

"I wouldn't want to mess with 'em, for sure," Ford said.

Jim, thinking grimly of the deadly weapons, hoped that Ford's talk about trying to steal the money was just that, talk.

After breakfast one day Ford led his horse over to where Jim was saddling up. "Any time now," Ford said under his breath.

Jim darted a glance at the others. Some were still at the fire, drinking the last of the coffee. Billy Coyle was walking over to where the horses were picketed. Jennings said something to him and Coyle laughed. Dark-bearded Sid Reivers picked up his saddle.

Jim whispered to his brother, "How the hell do you figure to do it without us getting killed?"

"Leave it to me, kid."

"You're not forgetting the shotguns?"

Ford gave him a tight smile. Across the way Cale Harper and Trent were starting to load the money sacks on the burros. "Think I'll go give 'em a hand," said Ford.

Ford went first over and helped Doc Thorne saddle up his horse. Thorne had ridden the chuck wagon on the way up and now forking a saddle on the homeward trip, seemed to have about done him in. He thanked Ford for the help. Ford waved a hand and walked over to where Harper and Trent were loading the money sacks. Ford pitched in and did most of the heavy work and Harper muttered his appreciation.

"We got a lot of miles yet," the foreman said. "Glad to see everybody pitchin' in."

Jim kept a wary eye on his brother all day, but Ford made no move.

The next morning Doc Thorne made hotcakes and cooked the rest of the sidemeat they had purchased in Abilene. The coffee was "strong enough to melt nails," Sandy Burkhardt laughed. Jennings and Billy Coyle, who had been on guard since midnight, rode in and helped themselves. After breakfast Ford busied himself around the camp, giving first one man a hand then another. It seemed that he couldn't do enough.

"Hey, you tryin' to get my job?" Harper laughed.

"Feel good this mornin', is all, Gale," Ford smiled.

Bascom Trent, holding a tin of coffee in his large hand, scowled at Ford. "The Norcross brothers sure act like little angels," he grunted. He turned his head and said something to Harper that Jim couldn't hear. Harper replied, "Hell, no, they're all right. I told you to make it up with Jim. It's just plain stupid, you two fellas fightin' over a gal who's already married to somebody else."

"I'm not talkin' about a fight over a gal."

Harper turned away from Trent and went to help Burkhardt tighten a pack lash. Jim was giving Doc Thorne a hand with the cooking gear. Ford went over to load Harper's own bedroll on one of the burros.

Harper said over his shoulder to Ford, "Looks like you're doin' half the work around camp." Jim noticed that Harper seemed mighty pleased. How long would this last? Jim wondered.

The burros were loaded and the men ready to mount their horses when Ford strode to the center of the campsite, and stood facing the eight other men, one of the sawed-off shotguns resting in his steady hands. Ford said easily, "Get your hands up, boys. Or your heads'll be rollin' in the dust!"

A shocked silence followed as the men stared, apprehension in some eyes, a gathering rage in others.

Even Jim had been taken by surprise. He stood paralyzed, with his hand still on the saddle horn, ready to mount. He hadn't really believed Ford would try it. But now he had, and Jim didn't see that he had much choice about whether to get involved now. They both were committed all the way by Ford's sudden act.

Cale Harper was the first to react. "What's the idea, Ford?" the foreman demanded in a tight voice. Jim, who was beginning to take in the situation, thought that was a damn fool question—anyone could tell what Ford's idea was just by looking at the shotgun in his hands.

"The idea is we ain't goin' on with you," Ford said. "Neither is the money."

"Goddammit that's why you been fussin' around everybody's gear. To get one of those shotguns." Harper looked around. "Where's the other one?"

"*I* got it!" Doc Thorne bared his teeth so that his gold tooth glinted in the morning sun. He held the second shotgun in gnarled hands.

"But it ain't loaded," Ford said with a tight grin.

Doc Thorne broke the weapon open. "He's right, Cale," the rancher said in disgust.

Bascom Trent began to swear. "Goddammit, Harper, if that Greener had been in my pack, Ford wouldn't ever have got his hands on it."

"Too late now," Harper said, with a shake of his head. "Now you see here, Ford . . ."

Ford said, "All right, shuck them gunbelts. *All* of you!" Ford noticed Jim, still standing beside his horse as if frozen. "Jim, get over here. Cover 'em!"

Jim drew his pistol and edged over toward his brother, facing the others.

Harper looked at him with faint surprise. "I didn't figure you'd be in on this, Jim."

"Reckon I am," Jim heard himself say. He looked at Ford a little dubiously, but Ford was ceasely watching the others.

"I'll be damned," Harper grunted as he shifted his gaze from one to the other men. "The Norcross brothers. If you think you'll get away with this, you better think again! The sheriff outa Abilene will be on your trail pronto."

"Take you some days to fetch him." Ford spoke so confidently that Jim had to grudgingly admire his brother's nerve. Jim himself was bathed in cold sweat. Ford said, "By the time you get the sheriff we'll be halfway to the border."

"You'll never make Mexico," Harper said.

Ford gestured with the shotgun, "I don't aim to tell you again. Drop them gunbelts. Then shuck your clothes!"

Sandy Burkhardt protested, "You can't leave us out here bare nekkid."

"Reckon you didn't hear me." Ford sounded tough. "If your hearin' don't improve we'll leave you here in a hole in the ground."

Gingerly the men unfastened their gunbelts. Ford told them to back off, away from the weapons on the ground. Ford turned to Jim, "Pick up their guns. Get their rifles. Run a rope through the trigger guards and tie them onto one of those hosses." The men grudgingly stripped to their long-johns while Jim hooked all the weapons together and tied them to a saddle horn.

Ford said, "Mebby we oughta peel these gents down to their bare hides." He laughed.

"You could leave them their underwear, Ford," Jim said. "Wouldn't hurt nothin'."

"But no boots or socks. You heard me!" Ford shouted.

He made the men throw their boots and clothing into a pile. Then he and Jim warily gathered the clothing into a bundle and roped it to another horse. Just then, as Ford's attention was distracted from the group, Sandy Burkhardt suddenly shouted, "You ain't stealin' my share of that money!" He dragged up a short-barreled pistol hidden under his long-johns.

Barely had sunlight flickered on the barrel of the pistol when Ford drew his .44 and fired. Burkhardt staggered. The gunshot echoed in the morning stillness. The horses whinneyed nervously. The men stood frozen as Burkhardt sank slowly to his knees, dropping the pistol. Ford picked up the weapon and stepped back.

Jim watched as Burkhardt fell on his face and slowly rolled over. There was blood leaking from the rancher's smashed shoulder.

Jim turned to Ford, "Why did you have to do that?"

"Hell, kid, you saw him draw down on me. He'd have killed us. Better get used to it. You'll see worse'n this before your life is done."

Burkhardt lifted his head from the ground to stare at Ford. He cursed in a muffled voice, then fell back unconscious.

Harper shook his fist at the Norcross brothers. "I'll see you two hang if Sandy dies."

"He ain't dead," Ford said gruffly. The sight of the men standing in their bare feet and their underwear seemed to restore some of Ford's good humor. "You hombres are a sight, damn if you ain't."

Trent took a menacing pace forward. "I'll get you for this! Both of you!" His angry gaze settled on Jim.

Ford shifted the shotgun back to his right hand. Harper said from a corner of his mouth, "Don't rile 'em, Bascom."

Jim watched his brother. For a terrifying moment he thought Ford was going to cut loose with the shotgun. Harper telling Trent to ease off had probably saved his life.

"You fellas stretch out on the ground," Ford said. "Face down. First one lifts his head will have it blown off." He told Jim to search them to make sure no one else had a hideout.

Jim hesitantly felt along the rigid bodies of the eight men. He glanced at Burkhardt who still had not stirred. It seemed the bleeding was not as bad now. Jim hoped he wouldn't die.

"Okay Jim, let's get on the move," Ford said, and gestured at the horses and burros. Jim mounted up and grabbed the reins of the two burdened horses, one with roped weapons, the other bearing the bundle of clothing. Their strange loads made them nervous and Jim had to hold them close. The burros followed along on nimble feet.

Jim had ridden several hundred yards and when he turned to look back Ford was still watching over the men lying on the ground in their gray and red longjohns. Finally he heard Ford shout, "*Adios, amigos!* See you across the river in Paso del Norte!" Then Ford came pounding up, grinning.

Jim looked at his brother curiously. "Why did you tell them where we're going?"

"Don't be stupid, kid. We're not going to Paso del Norte."

When they reached the next rise, Jim looked back at the collection of cowhands and two-bit ranchers who were now on their feet. One of them was bending over the fallen Burkhardt. Jim remembered that

Burkhardt was getting on in years. He hoped that the shock wouldn't be too much for him.

Ford said, "Don't look so grim, kid."

"I wish you hadn't shot Sandy."

"We'd be dead if I hadn't."

Jim turned his mind to the task of herding the eight horses and four burros. After a few miles Ford called a halt. He glanced back and started to laugh. "Them hombres without even a hat between 'em."

"What are we stoppin' for? We should keep moving."

"Relax. I want to get rid of some of this junk first." Ford spotted a gravelly stream a little way off the trail they were following. They kept the shotguns and two rifles and put the rest of the captured weapons under the bank. They searched the clothing and took what was left of the cowboys' pay, then threw them on the pile and caved the bank in on top of it all. Ford told Jim to cut a wad of buffalo grass and brush out the tracks leading to the caved-in bank. When Jim finished Ford looked the ground over with a critical eye and muttered that it looked okay.

Jim climbed back into the saddle, thoroughly spent, still fearful that somehow Harper and the others would come charging over the hill and shoot them down.

"If we're not going to Paso del Norte, where are we going? What happened to all those grand plans for Mexico?" Jim asked Ford nervously.

"Later we'll cross. South of here they may be waitin' for us. If they manage to cut our sign at all, that is." Ford laughed. "Hell, kid, don't look so scared."

"I just want to put a lot of distance between them and us," Jim said, looking over his shoulder.

"Don't worry. I know all the trails west of here.

That guy in jail told me where to cross the border in Arizona."

Jim was surprised. "We going all the way out there?"

"They'll never think of lookin' for us in Arizona. An' if they do get close, it'll be their funeral, not ours."

"Let's hope," Jim said, and used a rope end lightly on the rump of a burro that had halted to nibble grass. He thought about how swiftly things had changed. Only a few days ago he had been riding herd on Arne Killebrew's steers. Now he was riding herd on Killebrew's gold, and with no intention of delivering it to its rightful owner.

Ford said, "Still worried about Sandy Burkhardt?"

"He didn't look so good. An' if he dies . . ."

"With your share of the gold," laughed Ford, "you oughta buy a funeral parlor."

"Why do you say that?" Jim demanded angrily.

"You go out of your way to hang crepe. Might as well make a dollar while you're doin' it."

"Goddam it!" Jim cried suddenly. "I wish I'd never gone in with you on this. Why *did* I?"

"'Cause you're sick of wearin' out your butt in a saddle twelve hours a day for Arne Killebrew."

Jim wiped a shirtsleeve across his sweaty forehead. "I still wish I hadn't turned outlaw," he said under his breath. He looked up quickly but Ford hadn't heard him.

"You better learn one thing, kid," Ford said. "In this whole wide world there's only me an' you. Nobody else matters a damn."

Jim studied his brother's tough face and thought, *Maybe even I wouldn't mean a damn to you if the going got rough.*

Chapter 4

As soon as Ford and Jim Norcross were out of sight, Harper went over to Burkhardt and inspected his wound. Fortunately, the bullet had gone clean through the shoulder. He tore a strip of material from the upper part of his long-johns and bandaged the shoulder as best he could.

Harper straightened up and looked over the strange crew. Six men besides himself, standing uncertain and angry on the gravelly ground in their bare feet. Harper shook his head and looked down at Burkhardt who was conscious but weak from loss of blood.

Burkhardt moaned weakly, "Them dirty snakes... them dirty snakes..."

"Don't talk, Sandy," Harper cautioned. "We got a ways to travel. You'll need your strength."

"Travel?" Bascom Trent said angrily, scratching his hairy chest through the front of his unbuttoned underwear. "How we s'posed to go anywhere in this get-up?"

"Well, we can't just set here and wait for someone to find us. We'll walk along slow and keep an eye out for chuckholes. Can't afford anyone bustin' a leg."

Billy Coyle looked down at his small feet. "I ain't much for walkin'."

"Me neither," said Trent.

"Didn't you blue bellies learn how to march in that army?" Harper snarled.

Trent reddened. "I was in the cavalry, damn it."

"You two was gettin' along," Doc Thorne said. "Lordy, don't fight now."

Harper said nothing. He knew he needed Bascom Trent more than he needed the rest of them. Trent, if he could be goaded, would withstand the greatest punishment, and would help drag the others along.

The wounded Burkhardt would have to be almost carried. They'd have to take turns helping him and it would not be easy to manage because of the smashed shoulder. Harper told Tom Cass and Trent to lift him up. Cass, overweight and puffing, slipped an arm under Burkhardt's good shoulder. Trent, avoiding the wounded left shoulder, put a long hairy arm around the rancher's waist. They started off.

Every step was agony for Burkhardt. After fifty yards he pled with Harper to leave him behind.

"Better to shoot you, Sandy, than leave you alone here," Harper said. "Since I ain't got a gun, you're comin' along with us."

Burkhardt nodded wearily and said he'd try to go on.

Before they made five miles their feet were so bruised and bleeding they could hardly stand. But they grimly plodded on, even though normally they wouldn't walk a block if there was a horse handy. Harper, in the lead, looked back at them strung out along the trail, an incongruous sight in their dirty underwear. He couldn't help but feel a certain pride in their guts that momentarily overshadowed his rage at being out-slicked by the Norcross brothers.

Trent hobbled up to where Harper waited for the others. "Christ, I can't make another mile," the big Texan grunted.

Harper was worried. If Trent failed him, the rest would quit. "I didn't like you worth a damn when you come to work for us," Harper said, his voice stinging. "I still don't like you."

"Who gives a damn what you like!" Trent said. "I recollect you tellin' me that the Norcross brothers was all right. Remember?"

"Yeah, I said that," Harper admitted. The others had slumped to the ground and were resting their weary feet. Burkhardt was stretched out on some grass. Harper worked over to him and checked the wound. There was no more bleeding into the makeshift bandage. That was good, anyway. Harper could feel his skin burning from exposure to the sun where he had ripped away part of his upper long-johns to make the bandage.

"Come on, boys. We ain't gonna catch those Norcross brothers sittin' here." Harper looked up at the sky. Dark clouds had blown in from the North. He thought of them caught in the open with no shelter. *Cristo!*

Trent scratched his chest as they limped along. His underwear was torn from brush. "Harper, you better start thinkin' up excuses for Killebrew."

"One thing the old man don't understand. Excuses."

"He'll hold you responsible for the money."

"Won't made any difference whether your pa knew the old man or not," Harper pointed out. "You'll get your neck roped to a tree just as quick as the rest of us."

"Mebby I don't figure to go back to work for Killebrew," Trent muttered.

"You quit and he'll figure you had a hand in stealin' the money. He'd even suspicion a *real* Texan," Harper added.

Trent's face reddened. "Harper, I told you to lay off me!" Doc Thorne, trailing on their heels, shook his gray head in disgust. "Stop it, you two," the rancher said wearily.

Neither man paid any attention to him.

Harper eyed Bascom Trent's angry face. "That's what I want, Bascom. I want you to get real mad."

"Well, you're succeedin', real fine."

" 'Cause if you get mad enough then we'll make it. You won't have no time to think about chickenin' out."

"None of *us* were yellowbellies! You're still riled 'cause our side won the war."

Harper nodded. "You just get madder an' madder. And so will I. If we hate each other enough we'll forget about rocks in the trail an' the long miles!"

"You're damn right. I'm mad enough to cut your throat!"

"You got no knife," Harper reminded him with a faint grin on his grimy face. Trent ran a hand angrily through his hair, then smiled uncomfortably. "We'll push on," Harper continued. "We'll find us some guns. We'll get clothes an' hosses." He paused. "Then we'll go after the Norcross brothers."

Trent said, "It'd take a Comanche to track them two in this rough country."

"Won't be too hard to pick up tracks of four burros an' the hosses they stole," Harper said.

Doc Thorne said bitterly, "Yeah, as long as it doesn't rain for the next month and wash out the trail." He eyed the dark clouds without much hope. Harper glared at the tired faces. "We'll find 'em 'cause we got to. If we don't, none of us ever better show our faces back to Texas."

"Some of that money was mine," Sandy Burkhardt managed in a weak voice. "Killebrew sure won't hold anything against me."

"You know him better'n that," Harper reminded. "He'll hold all of us responsible. I'd rather try to hold off a stampede with a buggy whip than tell Killebrew the money's gone."

Toward sundown more clouds rolled in from the north. Here in open country, with no cover save their underwear, they would be in a bad way if a storm hit. And at this time of year it could happen.

Doc Thorne hobbled up to walk alongside Harper. "How far you reckon to the next settlement?"

"No more'n a hundred miles," Harper said jokingly. But he didn't feel like laughing. The main cattle trail lay miles to the east. He remembered having been over this trail they were now following, but it had been some years back and now he recognized no landmarks. It had been his decision to take this less-traveled trail because of the gold. All around them it was the same brushy country and anything in the distance was obscured by the low-hanging clouds.

"If we don't get hosses," the corpulent Tom Cass panted, "we'll never last."

"We'll get hosses," Harper said angrily.

"Here comes the rain," Doc Thorne groaned.

Chapter 5

The Norcross brothers pushed on all day, stopping only long enough to water the horses and to let them graze a bit. A breeze came up and rattled through the dry brush on either side of the trail. Within the hour the sun was hidden and Jim felt the first slash of rain against his face. Ford kept the burros in line, heading into the storm, and it was Jim's job to herd the loose horses. Jim wanted to let the animals loose, but Ford said it was too soon. He didn't want to risk one of them drifting back to camp and giving Harper an opportunity to ride for help. Ford turned in the saddle to look back at Jim's discouraged form.

"You're doin' fine, kid," he said in a voice that was almost kindly.

"Wish I'd kept on heading north after Abilene. Got me a job somewheres."

Ford smiled; raindrops were chasing each other down his swarthy face. "Wait till we're settin' under a green tree down in *Mayheeco*. Countin' all our gold. You'll be glad you come in with me."

"Guess there isn't much I can do about it now."

"There sure ain't, kid. We're in it together, up to our necks."

Jim shuddered. To his weary mind the mention of necks instantly suggested a rope.

Ford said ,"You'll get over feelin' scared. First time a man is always gun-shy. I was."

"When was the first time with you, Ford?"

"So long ago it's hard to remember."

"I won't ever do it again," Jim vowed.

"You won't have to. We've got enough gold to last a lifetime." Ford smiled at the burros dwarfed under their heavy packs.

Finally the rain tapered off and the late sun appeared. Jim thought about the men they had left back on the prairie with nothing but their underwear.

"Hey, what're those guys gonna do if they run into trouble and them without a gun between 'em?" Jim asked. "It's dangerous country out here. If a man can't defend himself he could be dead quick."

"Their feet should be toughened up by now," Ford grinned. "If they run into trouble they can kick it to death." Ford seemed to think the whole affair bordered on the hilarious.

Jim wondered if he had ever really known this brother who called him a "kid." How could Ford sneak around a camp, pretending to be helpful, steal one shotgun, unload a second, and then throw down on men who had trusted him? And shoot one of them, an older man, a shirttail rancher who had joined the pool and was on his way home with a few dollars that just might tide him over for the rest of the year. Ford had risked not only his own neck but Jim's. And Ford thought it was funny.

"You shouldn't have shot Burkhardt," Jim said.

"Can it, kid," Ford snapped. "You should've found that hideout of his."

"I guess I'm new at this game." Jim gave a hollow laugh. "But I reckon it's the only game I'll have for quite a while." Jim had turned twenty just a few months earlier. Right now all those long years stretching ahead of him looked pretty bleak.

"Tell you one thing you likely ain't thought about," Ford said. "When that Nadine hears how you stole beef money right out from under Cale Harper's nose, she'll set up and take notice. Yep, females like her sure favor an hombre with guts."

"I don't even want to hear her name," Jim said shortly.

"That's fine you got her out of your system. I figured it might take a little time."

That night they made dry camp and ate cold beef and biscuits. Jim was too tired to miss hot food. Ford assigned him first watch so he put a blanket over his shoulders and sat on the damp ground, a rifle by his side. The horses on their picket ropes and the hobbled burros grazed a little and then were quiet. The stars came out, seeming so low that all he had to do was take off his hat and wave it to touch the nearest one. He wondered if down in Austin Nadine was looking at these same stars. His stomach knotted as he thought about how she had made a fool of him.

In the morning they had the same cold meat and biscuits for breakfast. Jim's nerves were ragged and he asked Ford, "If you're so sure we got away clean, how come you won't build us a cook fire?"

"Tonight we'll be far enough away." Ford was unshaven, his eyes bloodshot. He yawned, stretching his long arms. "Let's get them burros loaded, kid." He gave Jim a whack on the back jovially.

They were almost out of food. In all this time they had not seen another human being. Jim felt as if he had come to the end of the world. His stomach rumbled.

The next day, they saw a small settlement ahead, some low, unpainted buildings with sod roofs. Ford squinted at the smoke curling from a tin chimney. "I'll ride in and get us some vittles."

Jim didn't like the idea of being left a half mile out on the prairie in charge of the stock and the gold. But Ford said he'd be back directly and Jim watched his brother ride off, a solidly built man in trail-worn clothing. Just a drifter, if a man judged him by his clothing. A rich drifter, Jim thought, and eyed the packs on the four burros.

When three hours passed and Ford had not returned, Jim's apprehension increased. Just when he was convinced that something had happened, Ford came riding up, a rueful grin on his face. He had a half sack of flour and some bacon.

"Was you worried, kid?" Ford said.

"What happened?"

"Fellas had a poker game. I sat in for a spell."

"You lost, I reckon," Jim said angrily.

Ford began laughing. "Them three hombres would've died if they knowed the gold we got out here. And them sweatin' over two-bit cards an' tryin' to outslick me."

"What if they come after us?"

"One of 'em owns the place. He'll stay put. The other two are already headin' north."

"That was a damn fool thing to do, Ford. Leaving me alone out here. I had a helluva time keeping the burros from straying. An' they shouldn't have been made to stand around all that time, loaded up like they are." Jim didn't much care whether Ford would react angrily to this outburst or not. He was worn out with the long hours in the saddle and the worry that they'd get caught.

Ford gave him a long look, then shrugged. "Reckon you're right, kid. Losin' money ain't smart." That night, as if to make it up to him, Ford cooked them a hot meal.

The following morning Ford told Jim to turn the extra horses loose. Jim started taking off their saddles and bridles.

"What you botherin' with that for?" Ford asked.

"They could get hung up in the brush wearin' this gear."

"I see you're wearin' that halo again." But Ford seemed amiable and helped strip the rest of the horses. Then yelling and slapping the animals on the rumps he drove them off. Jim watched the horses tearing across the flatlands, manes flying.

"Satisfied, kid?" Ford said.

Later, Jim said, "Maybe we should have kept a couple of those horses. What if one of the burros goes lame?"

"Never thought of it," Ford scowled and glanced at the overburdened animals.

Jim, exhausted to the point of meanness, said, "I thought you had it all figured out. You're the one with all the experience at this sort of thing."

"Don't push it, kid," Ford warned.

"You're gonna get us stranded with dead burros and no way to pack that gold."

Ford swung toward Jim, one hand on his .44. And then just as suddenly he checked his temper. "I told you to lay off, kid. We got to stick together. Remember what I told you. There ain't anybody but us."

Jim looked around at the miles and miles of flatlands under the high scudding clouds. "You got any idea where we are?"

Ford either didn't hear him or decided to ignore the question. He stared at a silver coin he had taken from his pocket. "My *dinero*'s about gone. How much you got, kid?"

"Ten dollars." Jim had awakened that morning in Abilene with that amount in his pocket. He supposed Ford had "borrowed" the rest of it. "What about the pay we took off the other fellas?"

Ford shrugged.

"Don't tell me you lost it all in that poker game?" Jim was furious.

"Just wasn't my lucky day, kid."

Jim controlled his anger with some difficulty. "Ford, no more poker games till we get across the border, okay?"

"I got two weaknesses, kid. Poker an' the ladies. I swear off poker till we get to *Mayheeco*."

"And what about the other weakness?"

Ford chuckled. "Ain't likely there's no females in these parts that'd stir me none."

Jim had a sudden thought. He waved at the pack burros strung out ahead of them. "Why in the hell do *we* have to worry about money? We're rich. You said so yourself!"

"We can't spend any of them fifty-dollar gold pieces. Them eight-sided coins would stand out like a bull's-eye lantern in a root cellar."

"I guess you're right," Jim admitted. How ironic, he thought, to have a fortune at hand and be afraid of spending it.

"Sure as there's hinges on hell's front door, they could track us down."

During the payoff in the mail car, Jim had noticed that the coins were different but he had been more concerned with his aching head and Nadine's deception. Now he could see that if they used any of the coins to purchase supplies as they made their way west it would be like blazing a trail, with their initials on every tree.

"Don't look so down in the mouth, kid. Wait'll you splash across the ol' Rio Grande out in Arizona. You'll know then that it was all worth it."

Jim turned to look at his brother. "The Rio Grande don't go out to Arizona."

"How do you know?" Ford demanded. They were toiling up a long hill behind the tired burros.

"I've seen maps," Jim said. He squinted thoughtfully through the dust raised by the pack animals. "I thought you knew all about the country west of here."

Ford waved his hand as if brushing away flies. "So the Rio Grande ain't in Arizona. Don't make no difference. The border's still there an' we'll find it."

"They also got Apaches out there," Jim pointed out. "What if they try to lift our hair?"

"They try it an' they'll have buckshot in their teeth."

That evening Jim cooked supper, warmed-over beef and soupy gravy that he made out of the flour. They slept fitfully, taking turns on guard duty as usual to make sure no one jumped them. The precious packs lay hidden in the brush. By midnight a storm blew up. Jim, huddled with his rifle where he could watch the horses and burros, felt cold rain seep down the back of his neck. But the chill Jim felt was only partially due to the growing conviction that Ford didn't know as much about being an outlaw as he pretended. Jim wondered if in Ford's past forays, someone else hadn't done the planning. On his own, Ford was making fool mistakes, such as not keeping some of the loose horses in case the burros gave out. And worst of all was to get involved in a frontier gambling game. In country like this, Jim knew, a man could get his throat slit for a dollar. God knew what would happen to them if anyone ever got the idea that under those burlap-wrapped packs was a fortune in gold.

As they pressed on through the mud the next morning it seemed to Jim that they made precious few miles each day. A hill that looked distant at mid-morning seemed no nearer five hours later. To take his mind off his misery, he fell to thinking about what Ford had said Nadine's reaction to hearing of their daring robbery would be. Would she actually be impressed? And if he did become a big *hacenado* in Mexico as Ford promised, would she somehow hear about him and secretly wish she had chosen Jim Norcross instead of that older man from Austin? The one from the fine family, as Arne Killebrew had put it.

Jim's lips curled. To hell with her. She wasn't worth the energy it took for a man to say her name aloud.

Ford swung his muddied horse alongside Jim's roan. "What the hell you mumblin' about, kid?"

"Quit calling me kid. It gets on my nerves."

"All right, little brother." Laughing, Ford moved on ahead to hurry the burros up a twisting trail that snaked its way over a low range of hills.

Jim remembered how he'd see Nadine riding with one of the other cowhands and when he said something she'd look surprised and say that Bob or Frank or Ed or whoever just happened to be where she was. "And I rode back with him, Jim dear." And wasn't it nice that she hadn't had to ride alone. Jim had always agreed when she gave him that wonderful smile.

"How could I be so goddamn dumb?" Jim swore at himself.

Ford swung back from the burros. "Keep your eye

open for deer. I'm belly sick of that damned gravy. An' the beef's all gone."

"How long before we cross the border?"

"Be there 'fore you know it." Ford's voice, Jim noticed, seemed to have lost some of its former confidence. Jim wondered if Ford would be able to spot any landmarks in the country they were passing through. You could follow the setting sun and know you headed west, sure, but maybe that wasn't enough.

They might keep pushing in that direction until they came to the Pacific Ocean and that would be the end of Ford's dream of finding those green hills of Mexico.

Chapter 6

The next morning the sun rose over the distant hills into a clear sky. Jim felt as if some of the load of worry had lifted from his shoulders. Even though their progress had appeared to be agonizingly slow, they had, he knew, put many miles between them and the scene of the robbery far to the east. And each hour that passed without incident increased his confidence.

"There sure isn't anybody else in this part of the country," Jim observed when they reached a high point of ground.

"Nobody but us an' the buffalo," Ford grinned. They hadn't even seen many buffalo; just a small herd at a great distance.

That night Ford took first watch. Jim lay wrapped in his blanket and thought of one day writing Nadine, not letting her know where he was, of course, just to say he hadn't forgotten her double-cross. *But that would be a damn fool thing to do,* he told himself, as he stared up at a sky crowded with stars. In the first place, he didn't even know her married name.

Jim dozed off. When Ford awakened him at midnight the sky was overcast, the moon only a dull glow through the cloud bank. He took up his post by a cedar, rifle across his knees. For a time he watched the lightning playing on the horizon far to the north. When dawn finally worked through the overcast, the storm was still some distance away. But the air was sultry and smelled of rain. As the thunder increased the burros and the saddle horses began to grow edgy.

"Damn weather," Ford grumbled as he rolled out of his blanket. While Jim built a fire and made coffee and biscuits, Ford checked the burros for pack sores then loaded the gold.

Jim looked in the coffee sack. They had enough left for about one more meal. He hoped they'd reach some outpost where they could get supplies soon. And that Ford wouldn't risk any more of their dwindling supply of cash in a poker game. A particularly loud clap of thunder sent a shiver down Jim's back. It sounded to him like a hundred avalanches giving way all at once.

Ford scowled at the sky. "Just what we need—a little more rain." His beard had grown, and Jim thought he didn't look much like the jovial brother he remembered from his youth, who would drop out of sight for a year or so and then suddenly reappear. Ford was grim now—even a little desperate.

"It'll help cover our tracks at least," Jim ventured.

Just then, two mounted men herding twenty head of horses swept over the hill behind them. Their approach had been covered by the thunderclaps.

The pair of riders seemed surprised to come upon them so suddenly. And they didn't look friendly.

Their long hair and beards were filthy and they were heavily armed.

Jim glanced frantically at his rifle leaning against a rock some four feet to the right of the campfire. His holstered revolver was even farther away beside his bedroll. How many times had Ford warned him to have a weapon always at hand?

Jim tried to shout to Ford, whose back was to the riders, but his vocal chords seemed frozen.

Ford started to turn when one of the men shouted, "Hold it! Drop your rifle!"

Ford, gripping his Winchester, looked around. Jim had the feeling that Ford was about to chance levering a shell into the rifle. But at that moment a third rider appeared, a big man with a full yellow beard.

"You want to die right there it's all right with us!" boomed the newcomer, and Ford let his rifle fall.

Jim stayed where he was, kneeling by the fire, not that he could have moved if he wanted to. He had been about to reach for the coffee pot when the strangers appeared.

"Coffee smells good," said the one with the yellow beard. He kicked his sorrel and rode up to the fire. "We ain't had much to eat for two days," he said. He leaned over the horn to stare at Jim, then turned to look at Ford. "Who are you two hombres?"

Ford, recovered from his surprise, now seemed cool enough, Jim noticed. "Name's Johnson," answered Ford. He jerked a casual thumb at Jim who had risen to his feet. "My sidekick, Charlie."

"Unbuckle your gunbelt, Johnson." Ford did as he was told, acting as if this sort of thing happened every day.

"What're you packin' on them burros?"

"We're movin' to Mesilla," Ford said glibly. The

other two riders moved closer to their yellow-bearded leader.

"What you figure to do in Mesilla?"

"Goin' to ranch over there," Ford replied.

"Hmmm. How come you ain't packin' your gear in a wagon?"

"Country's too rough for a wagon," Ford pointed out.

"There's a fair road about five miles north."

"Didn't know about that."

"Or mebby it's too well-traveled to suit you." The yellow-bearded man gave a harsh laugh. He rode close to one of the burros and poked at its pack with a rifle barrel. The burro, thrown off balance by the prodding of the already top-heavy load, staggered. Jim noticed the look of interest that passed among the three strangers.

"You hombres must be purty rich," the leader said, "if it takes four burros to carry your gear."

"Odds and ends of stuff," answered Ford.

"You been mining somewheres?"

"Nope. We're cowhands," Ford replied. Jim had to admire his brother's steady voice.

One of the others, a lean man with an angry scar on his cheek, turned to the yellow-bearded man. "Lew, let's take a closer look at them packs."

"I'll do the lookin'," Lew replied and poked at the burro again with his rifle.

Ford said, "That's our property. You got no right to snoop."

"No?" Lew smiled and fired his rifle at the burro. The animal shuddered and then went down, the full weight of the pack pulling it over on its side. Lew's pale eyes were bright under the brim of a weather-stained hat. From the looks of them, Jim thought, the trio seemed to have traveled hard and far. Their horses were sweated up, even the loose ones now grazing a little distance away.

Lew was gazing at the dead burro. He seemed calm enough but the other two were jumpy.

"Shouldn't have fired off that rifle, Lew," said the third one, who had a hawk nose.

"Shut up, Hank," Lew said.

"We better be on the move, Lew."

Lew started to dismount. "We're not goin' anywhere yet, Hank. Not yet." He walked toward the fallen burro. "From the weight of that pack these hombres are either packing cannon balls . . ." He paused. "Or gold!"

The magic word caused the other two to rise in their stirrups to get a better look. Lew pulled a knife from his boottop and eagerly began to slash at the pack. The attention of all three men was riveted on what the knife would reveal.

And at that moment Ford yelled, *"Jim!"*

Without thinking Jim flung himself toward the rifle he had leaned against a rock before starting breakfast. As he snatched it up and frantically worked the loading lever, Ford was already crouching to retrieve his pistol from the holster he had been forced to discard at his feet. Lew, caught by surprise, dropped the knife and went for his gun, shouting at the other two, *"Get him!"*

Ford's first shot caught Lew in the chest and he collapsed beside the dead burro. The sudden commotion had set the mounts of the other two strangers bucking which spoiled their aim. Their shots went wide of the mark, one ricocheting off stones that ringed the fire, another slicing the ground in front of where Jim now lay full length, trying to aim his rifle. Just in time he shut his eyes against the sting of gravel. He fired blindly and heard a scream.

Opening his eyes, Jim saw that the hawk-nosed man had been in the act of dismounting, probably to get his feet on solid ground for more accurate shooting. Jim's bullet had struck him just below his left eye. With one foot in the stirrup, the man began to fall, and the horse, swerving, dumped him to the ground.

Stunned at the sight of the man he had shot, Jim lay on the ground, barely aware of Ford's second shot which actually followed immediately after his first. The bullet struck the remaining stranger in the stomach. He dropped his rifle, his arms hugged his middle, and he fell heavily to the ground screaming in pain. But even as he writhed on the ground, the man's hand slid toward the revolver on his hip. Before his fingers could touch the gun, Ford shot him again. The man jerked and then lay still.

All of a sudden Jim was aware of hoofbeats and for a terrifying instant he thought it must be companions of the three men coming in on them. But as he looked around, he saw that it was only the loose horses and the mounts of the three riders that had started to run. The spooked horses didn't go far before the grass proved too tempting, and soon they were grazing again.

Jim got to his feet and rubbed his cheek where the gravel had struck. He watched as Ford warily approached each of the bodies, his pistol gripped tight, checking for signs of life. He straightened up and said with a certain pride, "Dead, the three of 'em."

"Dead," Jim echoed in a hollow voice.

Admiration was in Ford's hazel eyes. "That was good shootin', kid."

Jim stared at the small black hole in the face of the man he had killed. It almost looked like a beauty spot. "Oh my God," he whispered.

Ford's hand clapping him on the back made him jump. Ford said, "When I yelled I didn't know whether you'd have sense enough to grab a gun or not."

"I did," Jim said absently.

"Good thing you did lend a hand, kid. I couldn't have dropped the three of 'em." Ford peered closely at Jim. "You're lookin' sick."

"I never killed anyone before." Jim's voice shook. He looked at the rifle in his hand, then let it fall. He knew Ford had killed many men in the War and probably a few more since then. But this was his first. Suddenly the nausea was overpowering and Jim turned and lost his breakfast in a thicket near the dead burro.

Ford mounted his horse and rode up the rise to where the strangers had first appeared. After scanning the horizon, he returned to camp. Jim was wiping his lips on a bandanna.

"You'll get used to it, kid," Ford said. "Our three friends was alone, I guess. But we better get outa here."

Jim agreed wholeheartedly. The smell of gunpowder still hung in the air. Ford roped one of the loose horses the men had been driving. The rest of the horses scattered as if suddenly they realized they were free. Jim noticed that all of them except the three saddled horses the dead strangers had been riding wore a J brand on their flanks.

Jim and Ford loaded the gold sacks the dead burro had been carrying on the horse Ford had captured. Then Ford went over to the still figures on the ground and began to methodically search through their pockets.

"Who do you s'pose these three fellas are?" Jim asked.

"*Were.*" Ford gave a short laugh. "You still feelin' a little tender about them hombres? They would've killed us when they found that gold. When we get to *Mayheeco* you'll be damn glad you done what your big brother said."

Jim turned his back and tightened his cinch.

"They sure didn't have much money," Ford grunted. "A few measly bucks. And this." Ford showed him a livery stable bill from Santa Fe made out to a Lew Tibbles. At least they knew who one of them had been in this life, Jim thought.

Ford mounted up and waved for Jim to shake a leg. Jim asked a little uncertainly, "Ain't we gonna bury them?"

Ford looked at him. "No time for that. They might have friends for all we know. This ain't no place to make a stand." Jim saw Ford was right; they would be vulnerable to any riflemen on the hilltops. "Now come on, kid, let's go."

Jim climbed on his horse and grabbed the lead rope of the pack horse with the J brand on its flank. The animal pulled back with such force the rope seared the palm of Jim's hand. He finally pulled the horse along at a walk.

Jim remembered his feeling when he first learned that he was to go north with the trail herd. Even though he had hated the thought of being parted from Nadine, he was excited about seeing more of the world than the Texas ranchland. Well, it had been exciting all right. In just a space of weeks everything had changed for Jim Norcross. He had fired a bullet into the face of an unknown man. He had been party to abandoning former friends far to the east on a perilous stretch of frontier. Not to mention robbing them. And now there was no turning back, because he was not only a thief, but a killer.

Chapter 7

Cale Harper was not a religious man nor did he ordinarily put much faith in prayer. But each morning when he and his men arose footsore and weary, he thought of the bloodied tracks left by their lacerated feet and prayed. His prayer was simple: that someone would come along with a wagon or extra horses. Of course there was about an equal chance in this country that anyone they met would be unfriendly. They might receive help or they might have their heads blown off. After all, Harper had to admit, they did look like savage wild men in their tattered longjohns.

Harper's shoulder and chest where he had ripped away his underwear to make a bandage for Sandy Burkhardt was burned and beginning to peel. And they were all covered with mud from slogging along in the chilling rainstorm yesterday. Today the weather had cleared somewhat, but Harper could still see lightning to the west of them. He added to his simple prayer: *Lord, hold off the rain today. And let me live long enough to ram a gun in the belly of Ford Norcross and watch him squirm.* As he thought about it, though, he didn't believe Ford would squirm. With his last breath, Ford would likely curse in his face.

Harper was not the only one with these thoughts. Each of those who had been robbed and abandoned by the Norcross brothers dreamed retribution with each painful step along the stony trail. A simple death was no punishment for a man like Ford Norcross.

During the agonizing trek across the empty land, Harper's grudging respect for the big Texan Bascom Trent increased, even though he had despised and ridiculed him not too long ago. Even at the ranch Harper had given him the worst jobs, hoping he'd quit. But Trent had stuck it out. Now he was the only one of the group Harper felt he could count on in a crisis.

The wonded Burkhardt was of no use in a fight. Old Doc Thorne's reflexes were too slow. Tom Cass was overweight and out of shape. When performing such a simple chore as pulling on his boots he would pant. The three other 77 riders, Rick Jennings, Sid Reivers, and Billy Coyle, were good soldiers and would fight if called upon. But they had to be directed. Trent was the only one who could think for himself, Harper felt.

One day when they paused to rest their torn feet, Harper said to Trent, "If something happens to me, I want you to swear to keep on after them two Norcross brothers."

"You don't have to worry none about that, Cale. I'll spend the rest of my life—an' I mean that—to get them bastards. The grudge I got against Ford is mighty powerful on account of what he done to us.

The one I got against his brother ain't no less, for hittin' me in the face when I wasn't lookin'."

Harper thought from what he'd heard it hadn't happened quite that way. Well, they'd all underestimated Jim Norcross. *Something he and Trent would never do from here on out,* Harper vowed silently.

Sandy Burkhardt lifted his head and called from where he lay on the ground, "What you two fellas jawin' about?"

Harper gave the wounded rancher a hard grin. "What we aim to do to the Norcross brothers."

"It couldn't be half as much as I aim to do." It was Burkhardt's hatred of Ford that had kept him going. Today Burkhardt had taken a few steps unassisted, which was amazing progress. Despite his drawn and shrunken face Harper knew he was going to make it.

The next afternoon as they came over a hump of ground, they saw ahead not only a road of sorts, but a one-story rambling structure of unpainted lumber, several sheds, and two corrals, one of them holding two dozen head of horses.

"Bonanza," Harper breathed as the men crowded up beside him to stare down at what appeared to be a trading post some hundred yards away. Except for the horses in the corral there seemed to be no sign of life.

Quietly they crept down the brushy slope. When they had covered half the distance to the building, a door crashed open and two men appeared, holding rifles.

Harper and the others continued warily down to the wagon road, keeping under cover in the brush. Then the bigger of the two men watching from the building shouted, "Far enough!"

His thinner companion, who wore a wide-brimmed

dark hat, leaned forward to peer at them. "They ain't human. Got to be animal."

Harper saw the two men exchange a few words. He couldn't overhear because of the distance, nor could he make out their faces shadowed in the doorway. He did see them lever shells into their rifles.

Doc Thorne had come to halt beside Harper. "They aim to drive us off," Thorne said.

"Gawd, look at them horses," breathed Burkhardt. "How would it feel for a man to get off his feet an' set his butt on a saddle?"

"We can't stand another five miles on our feet," Harper said grimly, as the two men in the building made threatening gestures with their weapons.

"Five miles," Doc Thorne groaned. "I couldn't walk a half mile."

Moving slowly so as not to alarm the armed men, Harper gradually edged farther back into the brush. "I'll circle 'round an' come in behind the building," he murmured. "Rest of you boys stay here and keep their attention."

"There might be another man inside," Billy Coyle said.

"Just have to take my chances," Harper said. He ducked low and began to creep along a shallow draw that led off to the east of the trading post. His men kept up a barrage of chatter to distract the pair below. Harper worked his way around to the side of the building, then rose to a crouch in a thicket and risked a glance at the men in the doorway. They were warning Trent and the others to keep away.

Harper took a deep breath. Here he would have to risk crossing open ground in order to reach the back of the building.

Trent was shouting now. "Let us come on in!"

"Not a chance. You bastards keep your distance or

we'll shoot you down and leave your dirty corpses for the buzzards." While they were thus engaged, Harper reached the safety of the building.

"Go on, clear out!" one of the riflemen was yelling at the ragtag group of men on the slope. "Won't tell you again!"

While he caught his breath, Harper glanced at his men, having to admit they were a bedraggled lot. He could hardly blame the pair in the doorway for being suspicious. But they were also getting impatient and he'd have to move fast. He began to explore the rear wall of the building, seeking an opening. He found a window, but the shutters were locked on the inside. The rear door was barred. Damn.

Trent was bellowing that they needed help. Again they were warned to stay back. This time the warning was punctuated by a rifle shot.

"Next time it won't be over your heads!" cried the big one in a deep voice. "We never seen the likes of you. Now you fellas git!"

Harper, edging along the back wall, let his admiring gaze fall on the horses in the corral. They would have mounts at least, if their luck held. Oh Gawd . . ."

The horses had noticed the strange-looking figure with tousled hair and ragged underwear, moving painfully on bare feet. They tossed their heads and began moving nervously around the corral. Harper tensed, knowing that any moment one of the riflemen might come to investigate what was upsetting the horses.

But there was more yelling out front and another rifle shot.

Trent yelled, "You tryin' to kill us!"

And at that moment Harper found another window, this one unshuttered. *Hallelujah!*

Without stopping to consider the risk if someone happened to be inside, he threw a leg over the sill, pulled himself in, and dropped to the floor. As his eyes adjusted to the dimness he made out a long narrow room with two poker tables, a short bar, and some shelves containing work clothes and tinned goods. The room was deserted. Through the open doorway he could see the pair in front of the trading post.

Harper looked around for a weapon. At any moment one of those in the doorway could turn and end it all with a rifle shot. He spotted a rifle on wall pegs behind the bar. His heart pounded as he moved quickly, ignoring the pain in his sore feet. He snatched the rifle off its pegs; it was a Henry. He worked the loading lever and heard a shell slide into the breech.

He edged around the bar and moved silently to the door. The big man was shouting, "We don't give a damn who you are. We been tricked before . . ."

He broke off as Harper rammed the rifle into his back. As he started to turn, Harper warned, "The two of you stand easy or you're dead."

"What the hell?" the thin one grunted in surprise. He rolled his eyes so that he saw the rifle against the other's back.

"Put down your rifles, easy like," Harper ordered. "We don't mean you no harm. We just need some help."

"I won't put down my rifle for anybody," the thin one blustered.

The big one said, "Ike, he's got the gun on me, not you. Do like he says!"

They let the rifles fall to the hard-packed dirt in front of the trading post. Harper waved for his companions to come on in. They came limping up in their long-johns and bare feet. Trent and Billy Coyle picked up the two rifles the men had dropped, then searched them for hideouts.

The big man, Larry Werther, peered at Harper's sunburned and determined face. "We figured you fellas was some kind of loco injuns."

"You can see we're white."

"Never seen white men run around in nothin' but their long-johns," Werther said skeptically.

Harper said, "You've seen it now," and motioned the two men into the building. His own crew stumbled after them. Some sank wearily into chairs, others to the floor, with their backs against a wall.

The thin man in the dark hat, Ike Todman, glanced at the rear window where Harper had entered. "Next time we spot ghosts from hell walkin' up on us in their bare feet," he grumbled, "we better lock up *everything*."

Trent limped behind the bar where he helped himself to a bottle, took a long pull, then passed it around.

Werther gave him a black look. "Mighty free with our whiskey, ain't you?"

"Best damn whiskey I ever tasted," sighed Sandy Burkhardt from one of the chairs.

Harper wiped his mouth and turned to Werther. "My men have been through hell. You can see their feet. Somebody stole our boots."

Werther stared at the blood smears some of the men had left on the plank floor. "Anybody that'd steal a man's boots oughta be hung."

"We'll agree with you on that. They stole our money, hosses, and clothing too." Harper went on to describe the Norcross brothers. He asked if a pair answering that description had been by recently. Trent started to mention the four burros, but Harper gave him a warning shake of the head. Trent nodded that he understood and fell silent.

Werther glowered and said, "Didn't see nobody answering that description around here." He looked at Harper. "Just what in hell you fellas aim to do now?"

"We'll need food, new clothes, supplies, horses, and money. We're gonna catch those two if we gotta die doin' it."

Werther said indignantly, "An' just how d'you expect to pay for all that? Or are you fellas outlaws like your friends who stuck you up? Why'd them fellas take your guns an' hosses, anyway?" he asked.

Harper had purposely refrained from mentioning the gold because it might give this pair ideas of their own. "Argument over the war," he answered with a straight face.

Todman was looking at Burkhardt. "What happened to him?"

"Ford Norcross shot him," Harper replied.

"All this on account of an argument over the war?" Werther said with disbelief.

"I don't give a damn whether you believe us or not," Harper said wearily. "But I tell you this. You've likely heard of Arne Killebrew. He'll feel kindly toward them that help us out. We're hands on the 77 ranch. We were just comin' back from deliverin' a herd to Abilene when this happened."

Werther's eyes were suddenly shrewd. "How'd you get paid for that herd? A lot of fellas these days won't take nothin' but cash money."

Harper shook his head. "Paid by bank draft. It's been mailed to Killebrew in Texas. Now, let's get down to business."

"You got any paper on you, anything to show you're from the Killebrew outfit?"

Harper patted the barrel of the Henry rifle. "This is all the paper I need, friend."

"I figured you was gonna rob us," Werther grunted. "Killebrew will stand back of every dollar you give us."

"We ain't *givin'* you fellas nothin'!"

"You can give us what we want, Werther, or we'll take it," Harper said evenly.

Todman started to splutter, but Werther warned his partner to silence and said, "We could have the law on you fellas."

Harper gave him a cold smile. "I'm askin' for help. But if you decide to send the law after us, I tell you this. The next Texas trail herd that comes this way will swing over and level this place. A stampede could sure run pounds off longhorns, I admit. But at the same time there'd be nothin' left of this post but splinters an' dust."

While Werther thought this over, Trent and Coyle started searching the room for weapons. They dragged out some chests from the living quarters. "Rifles, pistols, and shells," Trent said as he threw open the lid of one of the chests.

"I'll see that you get paid double for whatever we take," Harper said to the pair. He set his men to gathering up the supplies they would need.

When Werther realized they'd be taking eight horses he paled in anger. "Eight of my best hosses?"

"Maybe we'll only take seven," Harper said. "Should leave Burkhardt here . . ."

"The hell you will," Burkhardt interrupted before the foreman could finish. "I'm weak as sin, but by the time we catch up to them sons of bitches, I'll be able to shoot a gun." Harper, knowing how strongly Burkhardt felt about the robbery, relented.

Werther stepped to the bar and scribbled some

figures on a sheet of paper with a pencil stub. "You swear I'll get double pay?"

Harper nodded. "But don't pad the bill."

"Well, I'll take a chance on you fellas," Werther said as if he had a choice.

While Todman heated up a strong beef stew, Werther went through his stock of clothing and outfitted each man, all the while grumbling at the expense involved. The fit was not the best, but not one of the men complained. Getting boots onto swollen feet was the worst part.

"Hope you spread the word," Werther said, "that this place ain't too far outa the way to supply the Texas trail herds."

"I promise you this," Harper said, "Every 77 herd will come this way as long as I'm foreman. And I aim to be foreman for quite a spell." He took the pencil and on the bottom of the bill wrote a note to his boss, explaining the situation. "You just send this down to the Killebrew spread; an' you'll get your money right quick," he added.

As much as Harper would have liked to spend one night under a roof, he wanted to get started after the Norcross brothers more. Besides, there was always the possibility that some of Werther's friends might suddenly show up. Harper didn't trust these two and he sure didn't want to get into a gunfight.

As they prepared to mount up, Harper told Werther and Todman that he wanted them to ride along with them for a mile or so. Unarmed. "We'll leave your guns here so we'll feel safer," Harper said with a tight grin.

A mile and a half from the trading post Harper let the pair go. "Don't try and send anybody after us," Harper warned.

"I wouldn't do that," Werther said.

Harper smiled. "It wouldn't be worth all the killin'. And there'd be some on both sides."

"You got the stuff you wanted," Werther said. "And you signed the bill. Like I said, I'll take a chance."

When the two men started back toward the trading post, Trent said, "Cale, you oughta sell snake oil for a living. The way you talked Werther outa this stuff you could get rich."

"Wasn't my slick tongue," said Harper. "It was that Henry rifle I took off them wall pegs."

"Mebby they also heard of Arne Killebrew's powerful temper," Trent laughed.

Harper turned to look at his men strung out behind him. "How's it feel to set a saddle again?"

"Feels good to my butt," said Rick Jennings. "But when I step hard on the stirrups my feet hurt like hell."

Sid Reivers said, "Why we headin' north? Goin' back the way we come?"

"We'll go back to our camp where those two hellions jumped us," Harper said. "We'll try an' cut their sign."

"I recollect Ford sayin' he figured to head south," Doc Torne said. "And cross into Mexico."

"They didn't come this way or Werther would've seen 'em. They'll have to stop for supplies; we weren't carrying enough. And besides, if they'd headed this way we'd have cut sign already."

In a matter of hours they had covered the distance back to the camp. "Seemed like we walked more miles than there is between San Antone an' Corpus Christi," Burkhardt said.

The rainstorm had washed away all tracks from the deserted camp. But as the men searched in ever-widening circles, Sid Reivers gave a shout. There was a grin on his bearded face as he held aloft a small boot that evidently had worked loose from the pack of gear the fugitives had lashed to one of the horses. "Ain't this yours, Billy?" Reivers yelled.

Coyle spurred up. "By God, yes." Dismounting, Coyle worked off the newer stiffer boot from his small right foot and exchanged it for the old one. "Now I feel half a man again, anyhow," the diminutive rider grinned as he mounted again.

"You're all man anytime, Billy." Harper gave him a slap on the arm. "We know which way Ford is headin'. My hunch is he'll try riding a long slant southwest to the border."

They started west on what every man sensed would be a long chase. But their sore feet and aching muscles could not distract them from their single purpose: to run down the Norcross brothers who had made off with a fortune in eight-sided gold coins that had been minted out in California shortly after the gold rush.

Chapter 8

Jim's right hand was raw from handling the lead rope of the new pack horse. The animal did not like the pack and it was long past noon before he began to settle down. It was a good horse and would make a good saddler once they got to Mexico, Ford pointed out. The storm that had seemed imminent that morning and had helped to cover the approach of the three riders had passed east of them.

During the hours since the shooting Jim had glanced at his brother now and then, looking for any sign of delayed shock or regret. It looked as if Ford had put the incident completely out of his mind. He was whistling now, hat tipped low to shade his eyes from the sun that was now past its zenith. He herded the burros along, delivering a casual kick with a boot toe whenever one of them lagged behind.

Jim supposed that being in a war helped a man get used to killing. With men dying every day the taking of human life would make no more impact than a stubbed toe. Jim wondered if he would ever get used to violence, no matter how long he lived. Ford had displayed a coolness in the face of disaster that had been remarkable. There had been something in Ford's sharp and commanding shout, *"Jim!"* that had brought the inexperienced younger brother out of his trance and enabled him to snatch up a rifle, lever in a shell, and kill a man with a single shot. Even thinking back on the way the man had died chilled him . . .

Some days later they came to a river flowing through willows and grasslands. A Mexican woodcutter listened to Ford's poor Spanish and pointed south. "Mesilla," he said. The small dark man stood watching them ford the river. The three burros found the going difficult with their short legs and heavy packs. When they were on the far side, Ford pointed at a settlement of some kind barely visible through the willows lining the bank. It certainly wasn't Mesilla. The settlement ahead had only five or six buildings.

Ford smiled at Jim. "You take a rest here, kid. I'll go on an' get us some tobacco an' whiskey."

"We need food more," Jim said. "We're almost out of money, don't forget."

"Our three friends with the horses had a few dollars. Now you stay put an' I'll be back directly."

"Don't get in a poker game . . ."

Just then a man came out from under the trees and stood not a dozen yards from the pack horse.

"Hey there, you fellas!" Jim felt the blood drain from his face. The man began walking slowly toward them. He was about forty and was carrying a Sharps rifle and wearing clean range clothes. Off in the trees Jim could see a pinto lazily cropping grass. Farther back were other animals that looked like mules, but

Jim couldn't be sure. His immediate concern was the man with the big rifle who was advancing purposefully across the damp ground.

"Want to ask you fellas a couple of questions," the man said.

Ford scowled at the stranger. "What you want?"

Now that the man was closer, Jim saw no badge on his shirt. And the man appeared to be alone.

"Where you fellas from?" the stranger asked.

"None of your damn business," was Ford's belligerent answer.

"Don't hurt to be civil," Jim said to his brother. He looked at the stranger whose hard gray eyes were regarding him coldly. "We're from . . ."

"Shut up, kid!" Ford said. "I'll answer the questions."

Jim saw Ford's feet settle deeper in the stirrups—leverage for a fast draw. Jim's mouth was dry as he swung in beside his brother's horse. He hissed, "No need to shoot him yet! Let him talk . . ."

Ford waved him away, his eyes on the stranger. "Speak up," Ford said in a mild voice that didn't fool Jim.

"Just so there's no misunderstanding," the man said, halting a few feet from Ford, "my two boys have gone to the settlement. They'll be back directly so don't start nothin'."

"We're not lookin' for trouble," Ford said innocently. "Me an' my friend here are in a hurry. You got somethin' to say, say it." Above the trees some clouds were blowing in, darkening the sun.

The man with the gray eyes slid the Sharps slightly under his right arm so he could cover both of the mounted brothers. Jim, looking down the maw of the big .50 caliber weapon, shifted uncomfortably. From a corner of his eye he could see the shotgun strapped behind Ford's saddle. No use. He'd be dead before he could get it loose.

"What I want to ask you about is that Lazy J hoss," the man said, jerking his head at the pack horse.

"You don't like us usin' a fine animal for a pack hoss?" Ford drawled.

"That's not what I mean at all," the man said in a hard voice. "And I think you know it!" He paused, then continued, "That Lazy J hoss comes from up north at Creeber Springs. Belongs to a neighbor of ours by the name of Bishop."

"More'n one Lazy J," said Ford insolently. "You oughta know that."

"Not in this part of the country there ain't. My neighbor come up missin' over fifteen head of his best hosses a few days back."

"Like I said, there's more'n one Lazy J brand." Ford acted as if he might be discussing the weather.

Jim had a feeling the man was stalling for time until his sons returned. He was grinning skeptically up at Ford on the big Texas horse. "I'll ask you right out," the man said. "Where'd you get that hoss?"

"Bought it."

"Hah! Let me tell you somethin'. If it was the Tibbles gang that rustled them hosses, they wouldn't sell one hoss at a time to fellas like you. They'd want to sell the whole herd, not a single animal. You get what I'm sayin'?"

"You talk in circles, friend." Ford glanced toward the settlement, then looked back at the stranger.

"Or are you working for Lew?" the man said.

"Lew? Don't know a Lew."

"Lew Tibbles." The man glared.

The name stirred memory in the back of Jim's mind. It took him a minute to remember that was the name on the stable bill Ford found on the yellow-bearded man. So they had been rustlers.

"I got a hunch," the man went on, "that Tibbles sent you fellas in for supplies. An' I'd sure like to know what you're packin' on them animals." He removed one hand from the Sharps and gestured at the burros and the Lazy J horse.

Ford lifted himself in the stirrups to peer beyond the man. "Must be your boys comin' now," he said.

The man foolishly turned to glance over his shoulder, then realized his mistake almost instantly. But Ford, digging his rowels into his horse's belly, had ridden him down before he could recover. The man fell to one side, away from the thrashing hoofs. The Sharps went flying. Ford jumped down, snatched up the heavy rifle, and threw it over his shoulder into the river. He drew the man's revolver and threw it into the river too. The man lay sprawled on the ground, dazed. He shook his head and looked up at Ford who loomed above him, pistol drawn.

"You *are* with the Tibbles gang," the man gasped. A rumble of thunder caused Ford to jerk his head up and look around.

"Don't kill him," Jim said.

"I oughta." Ford sounded angry. "He opens that mouth again an' he *will* be dead."

A sudden movement off in the willows caused Jim to quickly draw his gun. But it was only the mules that the man had apparently been guarding while his sons went on into the settlement.

"Ford, let's get out of here," Jim said tensely. " 'Fore his sons get back."

Even as Jim spoke he heard the sound of horses coming from the direction of the settlement. A clap of thunder shook the ground and Jim saw the burros lift their heads, looking as if they might run.

"*Ford!*" Jim shouted above another peal of thunder, "somebody's coming." He could see two riders now, perhaps a hundred yards away through the trees. One was mounted on a roan; the other rode a big black horse.

Ford gave him an impatient look. "I see 'em." He swung into the saddle, drew his rifle, and levered in a shell.

One of the riders suddenly caught sight of the man lying on the ground. "It's pa!" he shouted. "Something's happened!"

The other one spotted Ford and Jim and yelled a warning. "Dave, keep back!"

As the man on the black horse tried to rein back into the trees, Ford fired his rifle. The horse stumbled, throwing its rider hard. The man rolled, losing his hat. He did not move.

The man on the roan horse spurred back the way he had come, firing a pistol over his shoulder. Jim heard one of the wild shots thunk into a willow tree behind him. Ford fired after the fleeing rider but missed.

"Come on!" Ford shouted. "Get them jackasses on the move!"

As Jim gripped the lead rope of the pack horse and prodded the burros into a clumsy trot the skies opened up. Ford stayed behind to cover the rear. Jim had ridden out of sight of the river when he heard more rifle fire back in the trees. His heart stopped. What if something happened to Ford? But before he could dwell on this chilling prospect, Ford came spurring up.

"Did you kill him?" Jim asked.

"Naw." Ford waved him on ahead where the trail they were following cut through a fold in rocky hills.

"You keep goin'. I'll cover us. If one of them bastards shows his head he'll have three eyes in it."

Now they had three new enemies, Jim thought. And maybe, small as it appeared to be, the settlement could get up a posse. God, was there to be no end to this?

That day they didn't stop for a noon meal, but pushed on. The pack animals needed grass and water, but Ford was unwilling to risk possible involvement with any allies the three men could enlist from the settlement.

"The Lord's on our side, anyhow," Ford grinned when he finally spurred up alongside Jim. He pointed at the dark sky, which was now behind them. "That rain sure helped."

"We won't always have rain to wash out our tracks," Jim said. Jim's right arm was tired from trying to keep the pack horse in line. At times the big animal was nearly as balky as a mule.

"Yep, the Lord sure smiles on us," Ford said. Jim looked at his brother sourly. Ford was anything but religious.

Suddenly a mule deer burst from a thicket dead ahead. Jim's nerves were so raw he almost jumped out of the saddle. Ford laughed, then spurred after the animal. But soon he returned to announce that the deer was gone and they couldn't take the time to track it down.

"No venison steaks tonight, little brother."

"What I'd give for a decent meal and a decent bed."

Ford made a sweeping gesture at the pack animals. "With that gold we can buy any damn thing we want."

"When?" Ford had no answer for that. He glowered

at Jim, then muttered something about scouting their back trail and rode off.

By the time Ford caught up with him again, looming ghostly yellow in his slicker, the rain was coming down again even harder. Ford grinned.

"They'll never catch us now. I even had time readin' your signs, kid. Nothin' but mud."

But Jim knew that rain or not, experienced trackers could cut their sign. Jim could tell that Ford also knew it by the wary look on his brother's face when he turned in the saddle on each rise of ground to search the desolate stretch of country behind them.

Rainwater cascaded from Ford's hatbrim as he turned to Jim and said, "Cheer up, kid. Luck's with us."

"I thought it was the Lord with us," Jim said with a tired smile.

"Same thing."

If being tired, chilled, and scared was what Ford called luck, then Jim knew he had a barrel full of it.

The burros plodded stoically through the waning storm, but the pack horse was still a problem. At each clap of thunder, even though distant, it seemed ready to try and kick loose from its pack.

"Next time we run into trouble," Ford said, "we'll use them shotguns. Nobody's goin' to get their hands on this gold. *Nobody!*"

Right then the pack horse shied at something in the trail, yanking on the lead rope with such force that Jim was nearly pulled from the saddle. He righted himself just in time. About all he needed now in this deadly game he and Ford were playing was a broken leg.

"Ford, why don't we just head due south?" Jim said, when he had quieted the pack horse. "I know the border is somewhere south of Mesilla."

"Them fellas at the river will likely figure we're headin' for the Mex line. If they go after us, that's the way they'll head. Seein' as how the rain took care of any tracks we left." Ford smiled, trying to act as if he'd planned it all that way.

"Let's not forget Harper and the others," Jim said. "We're getting a lot of enemies all of a sudden."

"Dead enemies if they get close."

Jim thought Ford's attempt at bravado was beginning to sound hollow. "I wonder if Harper and the boys ever got themselves some clothes."

"Only fool thing I done," Ford said savagely, "was to leave them bastards alive."

Jim was stunned. "You'd have murdered every one of them?"

"Should have, yeah. Made our goin' that much easier."

Jim couldn't quite believe what Ford had just said. "You'd kill eight men for a few sacks of gold?"

"We killed three since then," Ford pointed out. Drops of rain clung to his stubbly beard. "You kill three men," Ford said, "what's eight more?"

"I've stole money with you, Ford. I helped you kill Lew Tibbles and the other two. But I wouldn't have helped you gun down men we've worked with in cold blood."

"Not even Bascom Trent?"

"No."

"You sure punched him when he talked about the Killebrew gal."

"Punchin's one thing," Jim said as he shunted the pack animals away from cactus growing beside the trail. "Killin's something else again."

"Bascom sweet-talkin' your gal down by the windmill? You wouldn't take a gun to him?"

Jim gritted his teeth as old memories came crashing in around him—things he had been trying to put from his mind during their flight across the desolate miles. "I don't want to hear about Nadine!"

"Her an' Bascom, sweet-talkin'." Ford seemed to find release from his own fears—if he had any—in making jibes about the girl. "Well, that weren't nothin' to get riled about anyway. Half the young cowboys at the ranch sparked her. An' some of the older ones, far as that goes."

Jim stared at his brother's tough profile. *"You?"*

Ford lifted an eyebrow, giving him a wise look. "Was thinkin' about it when we got back from Abilene."

Jim didn't know what to say to that; Nadine would probably have tried to charm even Ford. He grimly repeated the drunken vow he had made in the hotel room in Abilene. "I'll never love another woman as long as I live," he said under his breath.

When the rain finally ceased Ford seemed to brighten up. A weak sun poked a hole in the overcast. Ford was saying, "Every year or so we'll get us a new batch of *chicas* down at our rancho. We'll have a dozen each, runnin' around our *casa* down in ol' *Mayheeco*." Ford grinned. "It'll be the life, little brother." Ford sniffed the damp air. "Seems like I can smell them green trees an' that good creek water clear up here."

Jim was hunched in the saddle, staring morosely at the tracks left by the burros. His hand ached from its grip on the lead rope of the pack horse. He was thinking that so far they *had* been lucky. They had managed to get the jump on Harper and the other hands. Later they had dealt with the three rustlers. And today they escaped from the rancher and his two sons at the river. But how much longer could their luck hold? How much longer before someone got the drop on them?

Ford took a look at Jim's glum face and laughed. "Kid, we got more money in them packs than the President of these here United States. Likely more money than there is in the whole of Abilene."

"We're rich, all right," Jim said, thinking of his tiredness, his empty belly, his constant fear.

"You know somethin', little brother?"

"I don't want to hear about it."

"In *Mayheeco* we'll have ten times as much. Money's worth more down there. We'll be *ricos*, that's what they'll call us down there."

"They don't call us that on this side of the line," Jim said with a half-smile. "Likely they call us sons of bitches. The Norcross brothers."

Ford laughed so hard he almost fell off his horse.

"We better call a halt damn soon," Jim said, "or we won't have animals left to pack that gold." He could tell that the burros were about ready to drop under the weight of the muddied packs.

"Reckon we should've took the time to steal a few of them mules back at the river," Ford said thoughtfully.

When one of the burros came up lame Ford looked more worried than Jim remembered seeing him since the start of this grand adventure. "From here on out," Ford said through clenched teeth, "we take whatever we want. Guns, hosses, mules . . ."

"And gun down anybody who gets in our way?"

"I tell you somethin', kid. When a man takes the big step he don't stop at one damn thing. Not one. We got ourselves a fortune. Now we got to get it across the border any way we can. If somebody wants to argue, it's their hard luck."

"Ford, we better risk takin' some of that gold and buy fresh pack animals."

Ford shook his head. "I already told you. We don't spend a one of them coins. Not a one. Not till we get across the line."

"We'll never make it."

"We'll steal some pack hosses."

"And have some more men chasin' after us?"

Ford snorted and gave a disgusted shake of the head. "You don't listen to a damn thing I say, do you? We take what we want!" Ford was standing in the stirrups and searching the country around them with worried eyes. He lowered himself into the saddle with a scowl.

Jim said finally, "You don't really know where we are."

"We're somewhere west of Mesilla."

Two days later, with the burro limping worse all the time, Ford muttered, "I figure we're in Arizona."

"But you're not sure."

"I got to admit I don't see them landmarks my *amigo* told me about."

"*Amigo?*" Jim asked. "You mean the man you met in jail?"

Ford shot him an angry glance. "I ain't in a mood for joshin'. If that's what you're doin'."

"I'm so damned tired I can't even think what I'm doing."

"I got me an idea," Ford said suddenly. "See what you think of it, kid."

Jim waited, konwing that what he thought would make no difference. Ford would do as he pleased.

"What we should do is bury the gold. Hide out around here somewheres for the winter. Nobody'll ever figure we're way out here. Come spring we'll dig up the gold an' cut for the border. By then they'll have forgot all about us."

"How do we live all winter if we can't spend any of this gold?"

"Mebby you could get a job clerkin' in some store," Ford suggested. "You know figures. You speak good."

"And what do you do all winter?" Jim drawled. "Set in some poker game losin' money as fast as I make it?"

"Or mebby we both could get ridin' jobs," Ford said, stung by Jim's accurate description of his propensities. "We could hire on for a few dollars a month. A rancher might be glad to get a couple of cowhands to help out."

"Where do we find this rancher who'll hire us on?"

"We go lookin' for him," Ford said.

Chapter 9

East of Mesilla the trail seemed very warm, then faded out because of the recurrent rainstorms. But even so, Cale Harper had begun to hope that the gold could be reclaimed in a matter of weeks instead of the years he was prepared to spend in running the fugitives to earth.

For some days now Burkhardt had been able to ride reasonably well, but although his shoulder was healing the wound had caused the arm to stiffen up. *Likely the rancher wouldn't ever be able to use it much,* Harper thought sadly. That meant that Burkhardt would probably be unable to keep on running his small outfit and would have to sell out to the 77 spread for whatever Arne Killebrew was willing to pay. No one around Saddleback was fool enough to offer a ranch for sale without giving Killebrew first chance to dicker for it.

On one of their long nights around the campfire, the talk turned to the War. Harper tried to change the subject because of Trent, whom he needed now in their quest for the Norcross brothers. But the big Texan joined the conversation and for the first time spoke of his reasons for joining the Union forces.

"I was just a loco kid," he said. "A friend joined up an' so did I. For the hell of it. We knew this captain in the Union Army—weren't really close to anybody on the Reb side. So that's how it happened. I didn't know what I was fightin' for. I was sixteen years old. Besides, the Union Army had blue uniforms and plenty to eat. The Rebs didn't eat regular, for sure."

"I hope the Norcross brothers don't eat regular," Billy Coyle said. "But they likely will. With all that gold they can buy anything."

"I got a hunch they won't spend any of that gold 'fore they cross the border," said Harper from where he sat by the fire, knees drawn up. "No eight-sided coins have turned up. Leastways so far as we know."

Trent rubbed at a faint scar on his cheekbone. "When we catch 'em, I aim to shoot Jim Norcross into small pieces."

"Glad I ain't your enemy," Harper said with a laugh.

"You was once." Trent gave him a level look across the fire. "I hated your guts."

"Likewise." Harper smiled.

At Mesilla they tied up their horses near the plaza and started a tour of the cantinas to ask about the two men they sought. At the third cantina they were beckoned to a table where a man with a swollen jaw was sitting.

"Pa can't talk," said a brown-faced young man. "His jaw's busted. But we hear you're askin' about a couple of hombres. An' from the way you describe 'em they're the goddam bastards that rode down Pa." His hand rested on his father's shoulder.

Harper said they were after the Norcross brothers because the pair had stolen horses and had wounded a member of their cattle pool. He refrained from mentioning the gold.

"Them sounds like the fellas," said the man whose name was Dave Kendrick. He and his brother and father had come south from their ranch, he explained, intending to sell mules at El Paso. The two brothers had gone to a small settlement for tobacco. When they returned to where their father had stayed to watch the mules, they found he had been ridden down. His wrist and jaw were broken. "We trailed 'em for a spell, but a damn rainstorm come up an' we lost their tracks."

"Show me on a map just where that was," Harper said eagerly. The bartender dug up a map and young Kendrick pointed out where the incident had occurred. He went on to say that three members of the Tibbles gang had been found shot to death east of there. Horses stolen from the Lazy J ranch had been scattered all over the country.

"Them fellas you're after had a Lazy J hoss too," said the second brother, a twin to the first. "We figure they're the ones that gunned down Lew Tibbles an' two of his men."

Harper thanked the brothers and asked the bartender if he could keep the map. Back at the campfire he and his men pored over the yellowed drawing. "I say let's split up," Harper suggested. "Four of us take the south trail, the others head due west. We'll meet here"—Harper touched a spot on the map—"at Wheeler Springs."

"If we ain't found 'em by then, ain't likely we ever will," Doc Thorne said despondently. "I'm about busted flat."

"Me too," said Sandy Burkhardt.

"We'll get 'em, boys," Harper told the two shirttail ranchers. He wished he felt as confident as he tried to sound. The West was a vast country and in it somewhere were two fly specks, the Norcross brothers.

Later that night when the others had settled down in their bedrolls, Harper drew Trent aside. "You an' me will go together. We'll take Coyle and Jennings. I got me a hunch Ford ain't headin' for Mexico. At least not right off."

Trent nodded. "An' when we catch 'em we'll string 'em up. I been thinkin' it over, Cale. Them two ain't worth a bullet. Jim scares easy an' I want to see his knees shake when I put the rope around his neck."

"Ford won't scare, that's for sure. He's one tough hombre. Even I got to admit that."

"He won't be so tough when his bootheels are swingin' three feet off the ground."

Harper shared the last of the coffee with Trent. He looked over at the others sleeping in their blankets. Burkhardt lay stiffly on his back because of the bad shoulder.

"Wonder how Nadine Killebrew will like married life in Austin?" Harper mused.

"She'll miss the ranch," said Trent. "Wouldn't surprise me none if she comes home visitin' once in a while. Without her husband. The boys—them she was fond of, that is—will be mighty glad to see her."

Harper frowned as he gazed into his coffee cup. "You don't make her sound like much."

"You *know* she ain't much, Cale."

Harper took a minute to reply. "Reckon I wouldn't even admit it to myself. Reckon Arne knew it. He may be her pa but he ain't no fool." He grinned.

"Guess Jim Norcross was really gone on her, though."

"Just before I hang him I'll tell him what a damn fool he was."

"I got a hunch he knows it already, Bascom."

Chapter 10

Ford decided they should try their luck in an isolated corner of the territory near a settlement known as Grayfork, which was surrounded by a number of small cattle spreads. They cached the gold in two deep holes in a patch of brush on a leveled off hilltop. Then they built a corral of brush for the three burros and the pack horse near a small spring. To try and stable the animals in town would be risky, Ford pointed out, even if they had the money to pay for it. If the animals somehow got out of the corral, they'd make other plans. Jim knew that the "other plans" would involve stealing pack animals.

They began to canvass the area for jobs. At one ranch Ford would ask for work, and at the next ranch it was Jim's turn. They tried four ranches without any luck. No one seemed to be hiring. Ford said he would go into Grayfork and put his ear to the ground while Jim hit some of the other small outfits to the west of town.

At a shirttail outfit close into the settlement, a young girl answered Jim's knock. "Pa's inside," she said, leading the way. Jim took off his hat, scraped his feet carefully on the doorsill, and followed her.

He entered a long narrow parlor-kitchen that reminded him of the place back in Texas where he and Ford had been raised.

"What is it, son?" asked a man who was probably fifty and who was just finishing breakfast at a plank table. He had been a big-muscled man at one time but now was a little shrunken with age.

"Was wondering about a job," Jim said. "Me and my . . . cousin." Ford had thought it would be better that they not be known as brothers. "We'd like work for the winter."

The man, who said his name was Sam Delaney, sized up Jim. "I got work needs done," he admitted, "but money this year seems almighty hard to come by."

Jim's gaze had strayed to the tall girl by the stove. At that moment she looked up and their eyes met. She flushed and looked away and Jim could feel his own face heat up. In his embarrassment he stared down at the cracks in his worn boots. "We'd work cheap, Mr. Delaney," Jim said.

Delaney glanced at his daughter who was nervously gathering up breakfast dishes, then said to Jim, "I can't pay the goin' wage."

"A roof over our heads and a few dollars now and then would be all we need." And Jim spoke the truth, at least as far as he was concerned. To sleep in a real bunk with a roof over one's head protected from the rain, cutting wind, or blowing sand. To eat a meal at a table instead of catching a few bites balanced on the heels beside a fire, a rifle always at hand.

Delaney scratched his jaw. "Where's your cousin now?"

"He went into Grayfork to see about work there."

"Maybe he's already found a job, though I doubt it."

"I'd rather work here at a ranch." Jim stole another look at the girl. "I don't much cotton to towns."

"Me neither," Delaney smiled. "Ella Mae, why don't you set out a plate for . . . what'd you say your name was, young man?"

"Jim . . ." Jim hadn't meant to use his real first name, but it slipped out before he could think. "Jim Peabody, sir."

"I knew some Peabodys in Westhope. You come from around there, son?" Jim shook his head.

Ella Mae, smiled at her father as she set out a plate for Jim. Her fingers, Jim noticed, were long and slender, the nails cared for. Nadine Killebrew had short, childish hands and he remembered her habit of biting the nails, sometimes to the quick.

"Well, I guess I'll hire you on," Delaney said. "You and your cousin . . . what'd you say his name was?"

"Lee, sir. Lee Masters." Elated by his good fortune, Jim rode to Grayfork to hunt up Ford. He found him in a saloon, half-drunk, and playing poker with silver dollars. Probably the money he took from the dead rustlers, Jim thought. He worked his way up to the crowded table and told Ford about the jobs he landed. Ford didn't seem impressed. It took some doing to get him away from the game. As they headed for the door, a girl came out onto the stairway leading to the second floor. She had yellow hair piled high on her head and she blew Ford a kiss.

"I'll see you again, soon," Ford grinned at her.

"Glad you won't forget me, cowboy."

Once outside Jim said, "I hope you don't get drunk

around the Delaneys. They won't like it. 'Specially the daughter, Ella Mae."

"Did you get her out in the barn yet, kid?"

"She's not that kind," Jim said angrily as they headed for their horses.

"Neither was Nadine," laughed Ford.

"I hope you're going to at least act like you want to work for Mr. Delaney," Jim said, ignoring the remark about Nadine.

For a week they labored around the home place, repairing the barn and the horse pens and hanging a gate. Delaney brought their meals on a tray to the small bunkhouse. But at the start of the second week Delaney said, "Ella Mae says we oughta feed you up at the house." He grinned at Jim. "I guess I'd like that too."

The next morning after breakfast Sam Delaney and the two "cousins" prepared to ride out together. As they crossed the yard, Ella Mae called from the doorway, "Pa's a hard taskmaster. Don't let him work you to death, Jim."

"Sure won't." They mounted up and Jim waved to her from the saddle.

That night after they rode in from digging out a water hole on the east range and chasing back some stock from an adjoining ranch, Jim complimented Ella Mae on the supper she cooked.

"Don't know when I've eaten better, ma'am," Jim said.

"I wish you wouldn't call me ma'am," she chided. "Makes me feel so old."

"Well, what should I call you? Me bein' a hired hand and all."

"I've got a name," she reminded. "How about using it?"

"Sure, Ella Mae." Ford had gone back to the bunkhouse, and Jim could relax a little. In the presence of this girl the tensions of the past weeks began to fade. He felt a sense of belonging.

On a Saturday night Ford slicked down his dark hair before a piece of looking glass nailed to the bunkhouse wall and said, "You comin' to town with me, kid?"

Ford put down the comb and shot a meaningful glance at his younger brother. "You better stop makin' calf eyes at that gal. You know we can't stay here long. We're headin' for the green hills of *Mayheeco* an' them sweetwater creeks. If we want to keep our hides we *got* to go there, Jim boy."

Jim sat on the edge of his bunk and chewed his lip. There was something he wanted to talk to Ford about—something he'd been thinking about for the past few days. But Ford was on edge now.

Ford grabbed his hat and strode to the door. He turned to Jim. "Well, are you comin'?" he asked impatiently.

Jim shook his head. No, there was still time.

Miles to the east a teamster said to Cale Harper, "Sure sounds like the two fellas I seen through field glasses. They had three burros an' a pack hoss."

"Which way they'd go?" Harper asked tensely.

"North and west of here." He waved a hand toward the mountains.

"How long ago?"

"Month, mebby five weeks."

Harper thanked the man and turned to the three men with him, Trent, Coyle, and Jennings. "Small world after all, boys."

"Let's hope," Bascom Trent said as they started on a sure trail again after weeks of search.

Chapter 11

One Sunday morning Sam Delaney came down to the bunkhouse and said to Jim, "Ella Mae was wondering if you'd drive her over to the Beauchamp place. It ain't a workin' day and you don't have to do it if you don't want to. You been working for a whole month and haven't taken time off like your cousin. . . ."

"I'd be happy to drive her," Jim said to the smiling rancher.

He put on his one decent shirt and wiped off his boots. He glanced in the cracked mirror and brushed his black hair out of his eyes. Was that the face of an outlaw?

When Jim emerged from the bunkhouse he saw that Delaney had hitched a team of bays to a spring wagon. Ella Mae wore a pink dress with lace at the collar and her pale hair was pulled back. She gave Jim a sweet smile when he helped her into the wagon. Delaney was sitting on a bench in front of the house, reading a copy of a Tuscon paper. At the sight of the newspaper Jim's heart skipped a beat. What if there was a description of the Norcross brothers with a list of their crimes? But as he climbed into the wagon Delaney threw the paper aside.

"I already done read this." He settled back on the bench. "You young folks have a good day."

"Sure you don't want to come along?" Ella Mae asked, smoothing her skirts.

Delaney shook his head. To Jim, he said, "Better take a rifle. You never know what might turn up in country like this."

"Right here, sir," he said as he held aloft the Winchester he had been given back in Texas, ten thousand years ago.

As they drove through the cool winter day Ella Mae pulled her shawl closer around her shoulders and said, "This is a real treat for me. I don't get to see the Beauchamps often. I hope you'll like them. Pa and Mr. Beauchamp don't see eye to eye politically. My father was an admirer of Mr. Lincoln. The Beauchamps are from Richmond so I guess you can see how they'd argue."

"I was raised on that kind of arguing," Jim said, as he drove slowly across a creek to avoid splashing their good clothes. "I've seen men beat each other up over the War."

"Pa and Mr. Beauchamp don't beat each other up," she laughed. "Couple of times a year they get together and talk each other to death, but that's all."

"You've had school, haven't you, Ella Mae?"

"Some. Then we moved away. We came here because it was better for my mother's health." Her voice faltered. "My father and I—we're all that's left."

"I'm sorry."

Ella Mae was silent for a minute, then asked "You went to school, too, didn't you, Jim?"

"Not really. There was an old maid school teacher where we lived. I had a crush on her once." Jim laughed at the memory.

"You sometimes sound Texan."

Jim remembered Ford's warning not to mention Texas or give any details of their past. "No, I was born in Arkansas." How he hated to lie to this girl.

"I've never been that far east," Ella Mae said. "I was born in Utah."

"You folks Mormon?"

"Grandpa was. But Pa sort of drifted away from it." They rode in silence for a while. A coyote bounded across the road a dozen yards in front of the them, causing the horses to throw up their heads, but Jim held them in. Ella Mae sighed and said, "This sure is lonely country. I get all on edge if I stay at the ranch too long. Usually me an' Pa are all alone there. And there's no one in town for me to visit. Do you have any brothers and sisters?"

"No sisters, just . . ." He started to say "just Ford." But he and Ford were supposed to be cousins. "No kin," Jim finished, feeling his face redden. He glanced at Ella Mae from a corner of his eye, hoping she didn't notice his slip of the tongue. But she was staring off over the desolate countryside.

"We had a church in town once," Ella Mae said. "It was a place you could go and meet people. But it burned down and the preacher went to Prescott to live. Now there's nothing much in Grayfork but cowboys carousing."

Jim nodded. Carousing was probably what Ford was doing right now. He wished Ford wouldn't hang around saloons using up their money on whiskey, poker, and those fancy women.

"I'm glad you came to work for Pa," Ella Mae said. "I declare I don't know what I'd have done for another long winter. When it gets cold and snows I feel like we're a million miles from anywhere."

"I'm glad I came to work here too, Ella Mae."

"You remind me of my brother in a way," she said, smiling. "The way you talk, soft-like."

"What happened to him?"

"He was in the War. The last letter we had from him was Vicksburg. We heard later that he was on a gunboat in the river and the Johnny Rebs sank it."

"The War was terrible." Then Jim blurted, "You got a sweetheart?"

"Not really. When I was younger I used to get crushes on the cowboys Pa would hire on for round-up. But most of them were drifters and Pa says drifters are no good. Oh, but I didn't mean you, Jim. Pa thinks a lot of you and I . . . well, I do too."

Jim turned his head and found her looking at him. The expression in her eyes almost made him drop the reins and take her in his arms. It was a feeling he had never before experienced, not even with Nadine Killebrew. Then the thought flashed into his head: *What would she think if she knew the truth about me?* He pulled himself together and pretended to be very busy urging the horses up a long grade.

"There's the Beauchamp place," Ella Mae said suddenly, pointing ahead at a sprawling rock and frame house set on a knoll. Already there were figures in the yard, pointing in their direction. When they recognized Ella Mae they started waving.

"The Beauchamp girls are pretty," Ella Mae said. "I hope you're not smitten." She laughed.

"Nobody's as pretty as you," he said, and she gave his arm a squeeze.

As they drove into the yard they were greeted by a plump woman and two hounds running about in the excitement of having visitors. "Don't let those crazy dogs jump on your pretty dress," the woman said. A tall man with a shock of red hair came from the house. Two daughters about Ella Mae's age stood in the doorway and two young sons were chasing after the dogs. The girls and Mrs. Beauchamp embraced Ella Mae and then everyone shook hands with Jim as he was introduced.

Beauchamp told one of his sons to put up the team, then he said to Ella Mae, "I see your pa didn't come. He still fightin' the battle of Chancelorsville?"

"Pa had to go over the books," Ella Mae said with a straight face.

Tod Beauchamp smiled. "Or maybe he wanted you and the young fella to be alone." He looked at Ella Mae's flushed face and at Jim's. Then, laughing, he flung an arm across Jim's shoulder. "Always knew Ella Mae would find somebody in time . . ."

"*Please*, Mr. Beauchamp." Ella Mae turned away to hide her flaming face.

The girls joined in their father's laughter, but Mrs. Beauchamp said, "Don't pester the young folks, Tod. Now let's all go in to dinner 'fore it gets cold."

Over the Sunday meal of chicken and dumplings, cornbread, and home-canned vegetables, the boys talked of horses and cattle and the Beauchamp girls wanted to know if Jim had ever been in St. Louis, which was positively the center of the world, according to the *Ladies' Book*. Jim said he was sorry to disappoint them but he had never been there.

Beauchamp said for his part he was mighty thankful that the Apache threat was over, at least for the time being. He asked Jim if he'd seen any sign of Indians in his travels. Jim shook his head. He wondered just how far he and Ford would have gotten across Arizona with the gold-laden pack animals if the redmen had been on the warpath. It seemed they had picked a good time to turn outlaw.

It was getting late in the afternoon when Tod Beauchamp said, "I don't like to send you young folks away, but I do believe you should get home before dark."

In the yard Jim shook Mr. Beauchamp's hand and lifted his hat to Mrs. Beauchamp who laughed and gave him a hug. "Lordy, you don't have to be so polite. Any friend of the Delaney's is a friend of ours."

Jim smiled but his heart ached. What he wouldn't give to belong to a family like this. He didn't even remember his own mother.

They drove off down the road, waving back at the Beauchamps who were still calling farewell. When they were out of sight Ella Mae said, "They all liked you, Jim."

"I liked them." He gazed at the distant sky which seemed bluer than he ever remembered, and tried to push all the ugly memories of robbery and killing from his mind. All that was behind him now. He would tell Ford tonight. Ella Mae slipped her arm through his and they rode back to the ranch in contented silence.

When they drove into the yard Delaney came out to greet them, lifting his half-moon spectacles. "The Beauchamps feed you young folks good?" he asked.

"The very best cookin' I ever ate in my life," Jim said.

"Better than mine?" Ella Mae said with mock surprise.

"A little practice an' you'll catch up," Jim said with a grin.

"Well," she huffed, and flounced angrily into the house. But she turned in the doorway and smiled back at him.

Jim winked at Delaney as he led the horses off to the barn.

Long past midnight Ford came stumbling into the bunkhouse after making a big racket outside unsaddling his horse. Delaney came down from the house, pants pulled over his underwear and carrying a rifle.

"I heard cussing and a lot of banging around," the rancher said. He eyed Ford who was sitting on the edge of the bunk and trying to work off his boots. Delaney sniffed the air. "When I was a young buck I used to try and drink half the town dry. Not all of it." Delaney gave Jim a nod and went out, closing the door.

"Sour old bastard!" Ford threw his boot against the door.

"Come on, Ford. He's been good to us."

"I used to take a belt to you, little brother. An' sometimes my fists. I can do it again, you don't shut up."

"Like to see you try. In your condition you couldn't hit a barn door." Jim joked.

Ford glared for a moment, then began to laugh. "You sure are in a good mood tonight. You must be gettin' somewhere with that skinny chicken you're so sweet on."

"I don't care for that, Ford! I sure as hell don't!"

"Wonder what that sweet young thing would think if she knew she was bein' courted by a murderer. You killed a man, don't forget, shot him dead."

Jim strode to the window and stared out into the dark. "He—he was a rustler."

"Mebby not."

"They were the Tibbles gang."

"We don't know for sure that was them. Could be

they was just three cowhands herdin' hosses. An' we killed 'em. *We* killed 'em, little brother."

Jim looked up toward the house. He could see Delaney just going in the front door with his lamp and rifle. Too far away to overhear, thank God. Jim turned from the window and said to Ford, "For the first time in my life I've got something good. I don't aim to lose it."

"Oh, yeah?" Ford mumbled as he flopped down on the bunk and pulled a blanket over himself.

"You take the gold. I don't want it."

But Ford hadn't heard him. "Blow out the lamp," he ordered, and turned on his side.

In the morning Ford was in an ugly mood and Jim wasn't looking forward to breakfast. But Ella Mae didn't seem to notice anything and smiled at Jim as she cooked flapjacks. As they ate Delaney gazed thoughtfully at Ford and then glanced at Jim, as if weighing the two of them.

A week later Delaney told them he wanted some cattle driven down from the mesa to winter grass. He drew them a crude map of the area. It would be a three-day job, he said.

On their second night, Jim was making coffee, his mind on Ella Mae. The cattle they had driven down from the higher hills were now grazing along a creek.

Ford, sitting on his heels beside the fire, broke the silence. "If you're serious about that Ella Mae, you better get at it. You an' me are pullin' out directly."

"Listen to me, Ford . . ."

But Ford went on as if Jim hadn't spoken. "I got directions in town about how to reach the border the quickest way. I aim for us to load the gold an' be gone." Ford winked at him and added, "I figure you got about one more week here, little brother."

"Cut it out, Ford. Ella Mae means more to me than that."

"I oughta beat some sense into you. I thought you got a skinful with that Nadine Killebrew. She threw her hooks into you, then cut you loose."

"I feel a heap different toward Ella Mae than I did toward Nadine. Nadine was the first girl I ever knew anything about." Jim stared at the ground.

"Knowed anything about?" Ford gave a nasty laugh. "Yeah, you an' about half the hombres in that part of Texas."

"Ella Mae ain't like Nadine."

"She's got about as much curve to her as a wagon tongue. Why waste time on a filly like that? I got lady friends in town who'll . . ."

"Shut your dirty mouth, Goddamit!" Jim had been been tending the fire, under the coffee pot. He was so enraged that he had to hold himself in to keep from hurling the pot, boiling coffee and all, into Ford's face.

Ford sensed what was going on in his mind. He drew his gun and said softly. "You touch that pot an' you'll have this gun barrel right between your ears with your head split like a melon."

Jim looked at him bitterly. "You don't give a damn for anyone, do you? Not even yourself."

Ford leaned back on one elbow, his other arm draped across his knee, the gun held loosely in his slack hand. "When the extra cowhands are hired on for round-up, I bet that Ella Mae samples . . ." he leered.

Jim jumped on his brother, their bodies crashing together with such impact that the gun went flying. They rolled over and over, then came apart and bounded to their feet. "You wanted a lesson! You'll get it!" Ford shouted.

The commotion startled the cattle and some began to drift, but neither brother was paying any attention to them. Jim met Ford's rush by smashing him in the face. Ford sat down hard, and stayed there for a few moments, shaking his head from side to side, his shaggy dark hair falling across his enraged face. He sprang to his feet, and Jim put him down again. "Where'd you learn to fight like that?" he demanded as he was climbing back to his feet.

"You taught me, Ford. When you'd come home from jail or wherever the hell you'd been. And you'd get good an' drunk and say, 'Little brother, I got to teach you to take care of yourself.'"

"Yeah, guess I did do that." Ford rubbed the back of his head and seemed to be thinking it over, but it was just a ruse. Suddenly he lowered his head and rammed Jim in the breastbone. Jim went tumbling, narrowly avoiding landing in the cook fire. Gasping for breath, he rolled aside as Ford tried to kick him in the head. Then Ford came down on him heavily. He hammered lefts and rights into Jim's face. Although Jim managed to block most of them, he tasted blood. Somehow he found the strength to suddenly arch his body and send Ford flying. Both brothers were up in an instant and Jim met Ford head on, landing a blow to the ribs and then to the temple.

Then just as he was set to connect with Ford's jaw, his brother backed off. Ford snatched his hat from the ground and dusted it off on his knee. As he put on the hat he jerked his head at the last of the cattle now streaming back into the hills.

"Well, there goes a day's work shot to hell," Ford said.

Jim lowered his fists, wondering whether Ford had quit because he was afraid he couldn't win or because he suddenly realized he needed Jim to help pack the gold. Whatever his reasoning, Jim was glad it was over, at least for the present. But he remained on his guard in case Ford changed his mind and jumped him. In Texas, Jim had seen him beat up bigger men than himself and hardly draw a deep breath. Maybe the Saturday nights in places like Grayfork were beginning to sap his strength.

The next day they rounded up the cattle, who hadn't gone far after all, and drove them back down to the grass. As they neared the Delaney home place at sundown, Ford said, "When we're in *Mayheeco* you'll forget all about this Ella Mae."

Jim made no reply. He stared at the warm lampglow in the Delaney windows. When Ford finally announced that it was time to pull out, Jim wasn't going to go along. Ford was welcome to the gold. Jim would even help him load the burros and the pack horse and send him off. But he never wanted to see Ford again once they parted. From here on out he would be Jim Peabody. Jim Norcross was dead.

Chapter 12

To a great extent, Cale Harper let his instincts guide him in his search for the Norcross brothers. He visited each settlement, no matter how small, even if it meant going out of his way. Occasionally they received heartening news. He and Bascom Trent, Rick Jennings, and Billy Coyle had kept to the north while the rest of the pursuers, Doc Thorne, Sandy Burkhardt, Sid Reivers, and Tom Cass, headed south. It was Harper's hope that they could trap the fugitives somewhere in Arizona Territory as they tried to reach the border. Harper knew definitely that Ford and Jim had crossed over the Arizona line from New Mexico.

The first place Harper and the others visited in each town was the saloons. From having worked with Ford for some months, Harper was well acquainted with the man's habits. A few times they received affirmative answers to questions concerning Ford. Of course he hadn't given his own name in any of the establishments but the reckless way he drank and played cards identified him. Some of the girls remembered Ford especially and had no wish to see him again. But so far, no one seemed to remember a younger man being with Ford here in Arizona.

At one point the trail swung north again, which puzzled Harper. Bascom Trent insisted that they must be following the wrong set of tracks. Billy Coyle agreed. "Hell, they wouldn't be headin' up this way, Cale. They'd be goin' south to the border." But Harper pushed on north.

A day later they came upon a trading post and blacksmith shop where the owner said that a man resembling Ford had purchased supplies. Another man, slimmer and nervous-acting, had stayed some distance from the post guarding three burros and a pack animal.

Harper's spirits soared. "Get your rope ready, Bascom," he said, and nudged the Texan.

"They sure weren't going for the border, though," the trading post owner said. "Course it's been poor weather an' mebby they got turned around. They was headin' northwest."

"What's over that way?" Harper inquired.

"Nothin' much," the man admitted. "A few two-bit cow ranches an' a town called Grayfork. Named for a fella called Gray who settled at a fork in the trail. Apaches got his hair some years back, though."

As they rode off Harper said, "I just remembered something about Ford Norcross. Even back in Texas, by God, he had no sense of direction. You turn him around twice and he's lost."

"Jim could keep 'em on the right trail," Rick Jennings said.

Harper gave a shake of his head. "Jim doesn't count for much. Ford runs everything. If Jim pointed to the North Star, Ford would argue that it was south."

"I hope they ain't lost that gold," mused Bascom Trent. "Makes a man itch just to think about all that money."

Harper turned in the saddle to give the big Texan a speculative glance. "Itch? Yeah, I guess that's one way to put it." The pair fell silent while ahead of them Coyle and Jennings were alertly scanning the hill country which lay to the north and west of them.

Chapter 13

Jim was lashing wire around one of the corral posts to hold a cross bar in place one Saturday morning when Ella Mae came up. "Jim, will you ride with me to town?" she asked.

"Can't do it," Jim said, as he picked up a pair of wire cutters. "Your pa set yard chores for me today."

"Your cousin Lee has already gone to town."

Jim glanced toward a pasture where Ford was supposed to be working. "Yeah, he's always sneakin' off." Jim was angry with his brother. Ford would lose them their jobs yet.

"I saw him leave," Ella Mae said. "Right after Pa started for the Beauchamps place this morning." She watched Jim twist another piece of wire around a corral post, and said, "I'd like to go to town and get some yard goods for a winter dress. I haven't been to Grayfork in ages."

"Thought you didn't like town."

"It's not much fun going in with Pa." She smiled at him. "Will you take me, Jim?"

Jim slipped the cutters into his hip pocket. "You sure your pa won't mind?"

"He likes you, Jim. He won't mind."

"I thought him and the Beauchamps didn't get along on account of arguing about the war."

"They have to work together to cut shipping costs. So it's really a business discussion. Do you know what a cattle pool is, Jim?"

"Yeah, I was on one once."

"Where?"

He avoided her eyes. "It was a long time ago," he muttered.

"You're such a mysterious person. In some ways I feel I know you better than anyone in my whole life. But sometimes it seems as if your past life has a curtain over it."

Jim turned away. "I'll go wash up."

Not noticing his sudden shift in mood, Ella Mae said enthusiastically, "Let's take saddlers. It's a wonderful day for riding."

"We'll have to tie on your yard goods behind the saddle," Jim pointed out.

"Fine. You can buy me a sasparilla and some hard candy," Ella Mae beamed and hurried to the house to change into her riding clothes.

Jim's heart throbbed. He would be happy to spend all his time with Ella Mae, even though so far he had barely touched her hand. As he put on a clean shirt he thought of his brother. He knew that Ford was set on pulling out soon, probably next week. There would be a showdown, and Ford wouldn't like what Jim had to say. But he would have to accept it.

He saddled up his roan and a bay for her. She appeared wearing a blue shirt, riding breeches, and a hat set on the back of her head. Jim held the bay for her and as she put a foot in the stirrup, she leaned close and brushed his cheek with her lips. Then, flushing, she jumped into the saddle. Jim felt as if his bootheels were two feet off the ground as he stood looking up at her.

"Did I surprise you, Jim?" Ella Mae asked.

"A surprise I liked."

Laughing, she spurred away, around the barn and to the town road. When Jim caught up with her they slowed to a walk, stirrups touching. Never in his life had Jim felt so at peace with the world. He was sure of his future now. He'd work hard for Delaney and maybe he'd earn enough to buy his own ranch and make a good life for Ella Mae and himself.

Because it was Saturday, Grayfork was crowded with rigs and saddle horses. Ranchers and plump matrons and cowhands in silk shirts paraded up and down the walks. Jim tied their horses up in front of the Grayfork Store.

Ella Mae beckoned to him. "Will you help me pick out some yard goods? Or are you like most cowboys and want to go to the saloon? If so, I'll wait for you here when I'm done."

Jim shook his head. "I'd rather be with you."

Ella Mae was delighted and clung to his arm. "I want to make something bright even though it's for winter."

"You look pretty in anything," Jim said.

As they started up the steps to the store he glimpsed Ford in the crowd. Ford was weaving a little, hat slanted on his head, with a girl in a green dress hanging onto his arm. Jim thought it was the same girl he had seen that day on the saloon stairway, but he couldn't be sure.

Ella Mae had also spotted Ford. She said, "There's your cousin Lee."

"Yeah."

"I don't remember seeing that girl around town before. Who is she, Jim?"

"Nobody you'd want to know." Jim tried to steer Ella Mae into the store, but she hung back, staring.

Ford saw them together. He gave Ella Mae a reluctant tip of the hat and the girl with him scowled. Then Ford said something to the girl and she laughed.

Ella Mae said, "It's sometimes hard for me to realize that you two are kin. But I guess it's not as if you were brothers. Are you very closely related, Jim?"

"No," Jim said in a taut voice, avoiding her eyes so that she couldn't read the lie.

The girl with Ford looked back at Ella Mae. "Kind of skinny, ain't she?"

"I been tellin' Jim that." Ford shoved his way through the Saturday crowd and with the girl on his arm entered the Grayfork Saloon.

She said, "Will I see you later, honey?"

But Ford's gaze was riveted on a stocky dark-haired man at the bar. Cale Harper. And beside him was Bascom Trent.

Harper was talking to one of the barkeeps. The bald man was nodding. At that moment he looked across Harper's heavy shoulder and right at Ford standing by the door. The barkeep pointed and said something to Harper. Harper swung around just as Ford knocked the girl aside with one hand and drew his revolver with the other.

A man at a poker table cried, "Look out, boys!" as Ford fired wildly and dashed out of the saloon. Trent and Harper drew their weapons and other men struggled desperately to get out of the line of fire. A girl screamed. The two men tried to make their way across the crowded room.

Harper bellowed, "Jennings! Coyle! *We got Ford!*"

Outside on the walk there was more screaming as women saw Ford with the pistol in his hand.

Coming along the street, dodging saddlers and wagons, were Rick Jennings and Billy Coyle. Coyle caught sight of Ford and took aim with his Remington. But before Coyle could pull the trigger, Ford shot him. Coyle went down, rolling in the dust. Jennings fired but the shot went wild and struck a metal sign above the saloon doors with a clang. A girl peering out an upstairs window quickly yanked her head back inside.

A man cried, "Hold your fire! There's women an' kids in town!"

Quickly Ford's experienced eye swept the plunging horses tied to the hitching post in front of the saloon. He grabbed the reins of a big Morgan horse, and bounded into the saddle.

Somebody yelled hysterically, "That's my hoss! He's stealin' my hoss!"

The big animal wheeled and reared. Its rump struck a buckboard wheel and it nearly went down. Ford righted the animal and fired back into the crowd of men around the saloon doors. A man dropped, his shirt-front reddening.

As Ford dug his spurs into the horse's sides, Cale Harper reached the doors. Leaping across the man Ford had shot, Harper lifted a rifle and fired at Ford's departing back. At that moment the horse swerved and the bullet lodged in Ford's right side. Ford collapsed over the horn and for an instant seemed about to fall. Then he regained his balance.

"Jim, Jim!" Ford shouted as he approached the

Grayfork Store where more people were milling about, wide-eyed. "They found us! Ride for your life!"

At the sound of the gunfire Jim and Ella Mae had come to the doorway. Jim stood frozen as he saw Ford gallop by, a bloodstain spreading on the back of his shirt.

"Jim . . ." Ford shouted once more as he spurred the horse out of town.

Down the street Jim saw Harper and Bascom Trent. Harper was yelling, "The Norcross brothers!" He pointed at Jim. "There's the other one — Jim Norcross!"

Trent fired and the bullet took out the front window of the Grayfork General Store. Ella Mae jumped back, her hands pressed to her face.

Jim vaulted over the rail and onto his horse. A man tried to seize his arm as he ripped the reins free. Jim knocked the man aside and turned the horse into the street. As he reined away he caught a glimpse of the tears spilling down Ella Mae's face. He cried desperately, "Try to understand!" But turned away as he knew there was nothing for her to understand but the truth.

A hand reached for Jim's leg. Rick Jennings cried, "Your brother shot Billy. Damn you both!"

Jim kicked him in the face. He cruelly dug in his spurs and rode recklessly down into the crowded street. Two men were bowled over and the rest leaped from the path of the lunging roan. A bullet screamed past his shoulder and he heard the crack of a rifle.

Up ahead he saw that Ford had slowed, waiting for him to catch up. He turned for one last glimpse of Ella Mae, a slim figure in riding clothes, slumped brokenly where he had left her in the doorway.

Ford, ashen-faced and bleeding badly, yelled "Come on, kid! Keep to the rocks once we get outa sight of town . . . won't leave tracks . . . we'll swing north an' lose 'em."

Chapter 14

Harper quickly got over the shock of coming face to face with the Norcross brothers so abruptly. It was too bad that Ford had seen them first. But Ford was wounded now and wouldn't last long in the saddle. Ford and Jim hadn't had the gold on them, so that meant they had hidden it somewhere. The thing to do now was run them down and force them to reveal the hiding place.

Harper pushed his way to where Billy Coyle lay in the street. Harper knelt to inspect the wound in his right leg. Coyle said, "Did you get 'em boss?"

"We will," Harper said, He looked around. "Is there a sheriff or a doc in town?"

"Neither one," a man spoke up. "El Peterson at the store is handy with wounds."

"Get him!" The man went running.

An older man, somewhat gone to fat, cried excitedly, "The big one stole my Morgan hoss. We better get a posse."

Harper rose to his feet. "Let me handle it, friend. You'll only get yourself killed."

"You the law?" the man demanded.

Harper pushed away without answering. He strode toward the pale girl who stood weeping in the doorway of the store.

"Weren't you with Jim Norcross?" Harper asked her.

"That isn't his name. It's—it's Jim Peabody."

"Him and his brother killed three men east of here. And before that they robbed me and my friends and shot one of us."

"I don't believe you . . . They—seemed so good. At least Jim did. They worked for my father . . ."

"Is he in town, Miss?"

She shook her head. "He's visiting neighbors."

"Lucky he wasn't here. He might've got killed in the shooting. The Norcross boys are tough." Harper saw Jennings nearby and beckoned to him.

"Rick, you head south for Wheeler Springs," he told Jennings in a low voice. "If Doc Thorne and the others aren't there yet, wait for them. I got a hunch that Ford and Jim will head straight for the border now."

"Don't you want help trailin' them two?"

Harper shook his head. "Me an' Trent will handle it."

As Jennings hurried to get his horse, Harper saw Billy Coyle being carried into the Grayfork Store. Up the street a dozen riders were milling about trying to form a posse. Harper gestured to Trent and they ran for their horses at the opposite end of the street. "I hope that damned posse don't blunder into 'em before we do," Harper panted.

"You mean on account of the gold," Trent said, running at the foreman's side.

"Never know what a bunch of men like that will do if they get the idea we're on the trail of a fortune. Gold fever some folks call it."

"Yeah," Trent grunted, and they exchanged glances.

Chapter 15

Jim marveled at Ford's stamina. From the look of the stain on the right side of his shirt he must have lost a lot of blood. Tensely Jim glanced back at the town, barely visible beyond in the hills. Any second he expected to see riders pounding after them.

He swung in beside his brother. "You hurt bad, Ford?"

"I'm still alive," Ford said through clenched teeth. "We got to push on. Can't let 'em catch up to us." He nodded toward a creek that twisted through the brushy hills. "We'll head upstream. Lose our trail in the water."

"How do you figure Harper found us?"

Ford was already in the creek. "We stayed here too long, damn it. I told you a week ago we oughta pull out. But you was so lah-de-dah with that Ella Mae . . ."

"Shut up, Ford."

"You hadn't oughta talk to your brother like that. I could die, you know. But I don't figure to."

At that moment Jim wasn't feeling too kindly toward his brother who had turned him into an outlaw. He thought of Ella Mae standing in front of the store as he was riding out. "If I'd taken a gun to her she couldn't look more hurt."

"Hell, kid . . ." Ford leaned over the saddle horn and for a moment Jim thought he was going to die on the spot. But he couldn't desert Ford, not now. And even if he did, there was no chance to go back and pick up the pieces with Ella Mae.

An hour later, after pushing some miles upstream, Ford said, "We better stop for a spell. Help me down, kid. I'm weaker'n a sick cat."

Jim lowered him to the ground. Ford cried out. "Jeez, it hurts!" Their clothing was damp from splash-along in the creek.

Ford, lying on the ground, looked up at Jim. "Wish you'd never gone in with me?"

"I sure do."

"But if we hadn't run off from Harper an' the others," Ford said with a weak smile, "you'd never have met the gal."

Jim couldn't answer.

"You had a little fun, happiness, or whatever you call it." Ford grimaced. "We got anything for a bandage?"

There was nothing in their saddle bags. In the evening chill Jim stripped down, peeled out of his long-johns, then put on his pants and shirt again. His teeth chattered as he tore the underwear into strips, then pulled Ford's shirt away from the wound. Ford grunted at the pain. As near as Jim could tell in the dim light, the bullet had gone clear through. But the flesh was badly torn and Jim was sure he could see a white rib laid bare. He felt sick as he bound up the wound.

Ford gasped, "When we get ourselves that rancho down in Mexico you'll think it's been worth it."

Jim just looked at his brother, so tired and scared and depressed he wanted to die.

"We'll have us plenty of Mex cows to run, an' we'll live in a fine house in them green hills where there's so much water you can waste it."

"Ford, you talk loco."

"It's the truth kid. You'll see, you'll see."

Jim jerked his head around at a sound in the bushes. It was only an old cow that had paused to stare at the intruders. Having taken her look she ambled off down the creek.

Ford was saying, "We got to go back an' get that gold. Nothin' else matters."

"I'd give up every one of those fifty-dollar gold pieces if I could have Ella Mae."

"You're a bigger fool than I thought you was, kid. Help me up." Ford put out a hand to Jim.

"Sh!" Jim hissed. He had heard another sound. Dusk was falling fast and he could barely see the spot where the cow had appeared. The sound came again—a scrape of metal on rock. Jim slung his rifle under his arm and caught their two horses by the nostrils to prevent them from whinnying.

"What is it?" Ford whispered. Then Ford heard it too—a click of steel-shod hoofs on rock. Then a murmur of voices back down the creek.

They held their breath as one of the horses came closer. A voice not a hundred yards downstream shouted, "They must've gone on up the creek, Cale!" Bascom Trent!

Then Harper answered from some distance off to

their left. "Over here, Bascom," the foreman called. "We'll head for them hills yonder."

"Dark as hell," Trent complained. "Where's the moon?"

"Follow the sound of my voice," Harper called out, ever farther away than before.

With his heart pounding, Jim listened to the sounds of the two horses fade in the distance. Well, they were safe from Harper—at least for now. But where were the others?

Ford said harshly, "Gimme a hand, kid."

"You sure you can set a saddle?"

"We got to clear out before them two come back."

Jim had to admit that Ford had nerve. Even with the pain in his side and his weakness from loss of blood, he still managed not only to stay in the saddle, but to keep the big Morgan horse under control.

"We head back to where we buried the gold," Ford said in a low voice. "We'll swing north an' east, an' come in from the other side just in case them bastards locate our burros. But they *won't* find 'em," Ford went on, his voice gaining strength as he thought of the gold.

"I'd hate to run into an ambush," Jim said, peering ahead nervously into the darkness.

"Christ, you worry too damn much, kid." Ford gritted his teeth. The wound had stopped bleeding but he was still in extreme pain. 'We'll go cautious, so stop your frettin'."

With Ford in the lead they started out in the full dark. Jim wondered if Ford had any idea of where they were. For nearly an hour they kept their horses at a walk, trusting to sheer luck that they would not run into a search party. Jim was curious about why Harper and Trent had been alone. Surely the others hadn't gone back to Texas? They probably had just split up in order to cover more ground. And what about the people in Grayfork? Maybe even now there was a posse fanning out through the hills to hunt them down. He glanced over his shoulder as they started to climb a long, rocky grade. As far as he could tell in the starlight, nothing moved behind them.

"How you coming, Ford?" Jim called softly to his brother riding ahead.

"Don't talk. Voices carry."

"I figured there'd be fifty men after us from town. Where are they?"

"Shut up, kid," Ford whispered. "Worry about a posse when we see one. Not before." They reached the crest of the hill, and rested their horses in the lee of boulders that sheltered them from the night wind.

Jim closed his eyes, seeing Ella Mae's stricken face. What had he *done* to her?

As they started off again, Jim made sure his rifle was loose in the boot. How could Ford be so confident when the odds against them were so overwhelming? Jim was sure that eventually they would be caught. And then what? Would they be taken back to Texas? Surely they wouldn't stand trial in New Mexico for killing three horse thieves. It had been a case of self-defense, the Norcross brothers against the Tibbles gang. And since when was killing a horse thief considered a crime? Stealing the cattle money was something else, of course. And although Jim had not actually fired the bullet into Sandy Burkhardt, he was present when the deed was done. The law, he supposed, would hold him equally as guilty as Ford. How many years in prison would they get?

Then a chilling thought occurred to Jim. Would

Harper and the others be so enraged at the robbery and assault on Burkhardt that the prisoners would never reach Texas alive? What would Nadine think about it all, he wondered? For some days he hadn't even thought about her seriously. When she learned what had happened to him her reaction would undoubtedly be indifference he thought bitterly. To her he was just another cowboy, a fool young rider who'd had the bad judgment to fall in love with her and allow her treachery to turn him into a thief and a killer.

When they topped another range of hills he could see a yellow light far in the distance. Lamplight at a window miles away. His heart contracted. He'd had happiness for the taking and because of one stupid move he had thrown it all away.

Ford said, "You ain't spoke for an hour, kid."

"You told me to be quiet."

"Harper an' Trent ain't on our trail now or we'd have heard 'em. Damn wind is cold."

"Yeah. Seems like we haven't eaten in a week."

"When we get to *Mayheeco* we'll buy out a cantina. We'll eat an' we'll drink for a whole week solid. How you like that, kid?"

"Mexico. I wonder if we'll ever see it."

"After we get the gold, we'll be there in two days at most."

"Do you really know where the border is from here?"

"Yep."

"You thought you knew before," Jim said wearily. "An' you led us in a big circle."

"Don't forget that big circle brought you to Ella Mae."

"I wish I'd never seen her."

"The hell you do, kid."

"I've brought her nothing but hurt."

"She'll get over it. Same as Ruby will get over the hurt I brung her."

"Damn you, Ford, Ella Mae's a hundred times better'n that trash you hang around with."

Despite his pain, Ford managed a chuckle. "Sure, kid."

Jim's eyes filled with angry tears. Why had he ever agreed to go along with Ford on anything? He'd known since he was a kid that Ford was no good. Maybe his weakness in giving in to Ford was a sign that he himself was no good either. A vision of Ella Mae rose in front of his eyes. She touched his hand and smiled at him. In the chill air of the moonless night he felt the tears slide across his cheeks.

"I'd give eight of my toes for a drink of good whiskey," Ford said in a weak voice.

Jim cleared his throat and wiped his sleeve across his eyes. "You think we should rest for a spell?"

"Mebby."

They bedded down for a couple of hours then started out again.

"We keep goin' now, kid, till we get that gold." Ford turned in the saddle to look back at his brother, the movement bringing a gasp of pain to his lips. "Ain't nothin' in the world more important than that gold."

"You keep telling me that. I don't believe it."

But Ford wasn't even listening. He rode hunched in the saddle during the long hours, head down. Once, with dawn bringing a faint grayness to the eastern horizon, he slumped over in the saddle so far that his hat slid off. Jim jumped down and retrieved it.

Ford straightened up. "Must've dozed off." He

gingerly felt his side. "Sorry you got no long-johns, kid. Bet you're half froze."

"I'm all right." Jim, thinking back on his life with Ford, came to the conclusion that this was the first time his brother had ever said he was sorry for anything.

"Mebby I don't know this country," Ford said suddenly. "But I can sure smell out gold." He gestured at a hump of ground dead ahead in the early morning light. Jim saw a portion of the brush fence they had erected weeks before. He had to admit that this time at least, Ford had known where they were.

Despite his pain and the long hours in the saddle, Ford was alert and wary. He called a halt before riding in and from a brushy rise of ground they carefully searched the area with their tired eyes. There was no sign of a trap. Satisfied, Ford signalled for them to ride in.

They found that two of the burros had squeezed out of the corral, leaving only one burro and the pack horse. Ford used up some of his dwindling energy by cussing out the missing animals. In broad daylight, Jim was shocked at the drawn look on his brother's face. Ford said, "No way left but to ride double. Otherwise we can't pack all that gold."

"We could leave some of it . . ."

"We are not leaving a single one of them gold coins. Go dig it up, kid."

Jim rode a short distance to where they had stashed a shovel along with some of their gear, including the shotguns. He grabbed the shovel and went over to where the gold was buried in the sandy ground..

Ford came over to watch him uncover the first of the sacks. He wedged the stock of his rifle between his knees and cocked it one-handed. "I'll keep guard.

If anybody tries to jump us there'll be a lot of dead bodies around."

Jim dug up half of the gold packs. In another hole a few yards away, he found the rest. An animal had tried to get at one of the packs, smelling the leather, but had evidently been driven off. The pack had been ripped down one side and some of the gold pieces lay glittering in the sand.

Ford leaned forward to peer into the hole. "Gather 'em up, kid. Don't they look good?"

"We can't use that pack. It's busted."

"Put 'em in a gunnysack."

Jim dug in the sand with his bare hands until his fingertips were sore, and retrieved the loose coins. He put them in one of the burlap sacks that had been used to mask the leather money bags.

Finally he loaded the heavy sacks onto the burro and the pack horse. There were three sacks left. Ford said they should use the big Morgan for a pack animal and ride double on Jim's roan.

Jim said, "We ought to leave some of the gold. I keep telling you that."

"Do what I say!" Ford stood unsteadily on his feet and pointed the cocked rifle. "Don't make me shoot you." He aimed the rifle at Jim's breastbone. It was the first time Ford had threatened him with a gun.

Jim finished loading the sacks. Ford's saddle was flecked with blood, he noticed, as he lashed the packs tight. "There's one thing I aim to do," Jim said.

Ford glanced suspiciously. "Somethin' about that gal, I bet." His eyes were bright with fever.

"I aim to see the Delaney house one more time," Jim said stubbornly.

"A damn fool thing to do."

"I want one last look at it." Jim's lip trembled but he glared at Ford with determination.

Ford turned away and spat. "Oh, hell, why not. They'll never expect us to go back there. Come on, let's move!"

Jim helped Ford into the saddle and then got up behind him. He picked up the lead ropes of the overloaded burro and the two pack horses and they started off in the direction of the Delaney place, about five miles to the southwest. After they had ridden for about half an hour, Jim remembered they had forgotten the shotguns and the other gear. Ford would be madder than hell when he found out, but Jim wasn't turning back now.

Chapter 16

It was still very early in the day when they came within sight of the Delaney place. Jim dismounted in some cottonwoods that grew along the creek where it made a sweeping turn toward the horse pasture.

"Where you goin'?" Ford demanded when Jim started for the house some two hundred yards distant.

"I want to see the place close up," Jim said over his shoulder. "Maybe even get a glimpse of her if I'm lucky."

Ford was angry, but let him go.

Jim walked along the creek, keeping the barn between him and the house. When he was less than a hundred yards from the house, Sam Delaney suddenly stepped from behind a pile of lumber. The rancher, red-eyed from a sleepless night, leveled a rifle at Jim.

"Don't make a play for that pistol," he warned.

Jim, shocked by the rancher's sudden appearance, was unable to speak.

Delaney said, advancing, "I figured you just might come back. The posse said I was loco to think that."

"Mr. Delaney..."

"You come back to try an' kidnap my daughter."

"I wouldn't do a thing like that, Mr. Delaney."

"The Norcross brothers," Delaney said bitterly. "You two must be kin to Jesse James, the things you've done."

"If you'll just listen to me, Mr. Delaney..."

"I don't like to do this on account of Ella Mae. But I'm goin' to tie you up and keep you in the barn. There's a posse out lookin' for you, an' I'll just keep you tied up till they come back."

"Mr. Delaney, I wouldn't hurt Ella Mae for the world."

"Thank God my gal didn't marry you. She was talkin' about it and I was halfway listening. Now turn around, Norcross. All the way!"

As Jim started to turn he drew his pistol and before Delaney, slowed by age, could react, Jim laid the barrel just above the rancher's left ear. Delaney fell, dropping the rifle. By some miracle the weapon did not discharge.

Jim snatched up Delaney's rifle and revolver and ran for the place he had left Ford back in the trees. At each step he expected Delaney to start yelling, and Ella Mae to come running to her father's aid. Jim was sure that Ford in his fever and his anger wouldn't hesitate to shoot her down.

When Jim appeared, panting, Ford was livid and said, "Good thing you knocked the old bastard down. I was ready to put a bullet through his head." He gestured with the cocked rifle.

Jim threw Delaney's weapons into the creek, then helped Ford into the saddle and climbed up behind. He glanced at the spot where Delaney had been lying, but he was no longer there. He was probably hiding in the house, Jim thought with a sinking heart, awaiting an attack from the notorious Norcross brothers.

Ford turned his head and snarled, "You can see how much good comin' here did you. Delaney hates your guts. Likely so does the girl."

"I suppose she does," Jim said in a low voice.

Around dusk they were miles to the south when a steer suddenly appeared beside the trail. Ford dropped it with a one-handed shot. Jim butchered those parts they could immediately use and in the twilight they devoured the tough, half-roasted meat.

Ford had weakened considerably during the long push that day, so Jim stood guard for most of the night. Just before dawn Ford relieved him. When Jim awakened two hours later he started to gather fuel for a breakfast fire. But Ford warned that the smoke could give away their position. They ate cold beef.

This morning, Jim noticed, his brother seemed in good spirits. "You feel stronger, Ford?"

His brother grinned. "Gold makes me strong," he said as he nodded his head at the sacks on the ground. "Man just couldn't up an' die with all that on his hands, now could he?"

They started out again. Water was scarce in the country they were riding through now, and there was little cover. Jim, shading his eyes against the strong sun, looked for riders. But he saw none.

Ford kept the rifle in the boot cocked. Their pace on the single horse was a slow walk and both brothers were edgy. Several times Jim suggested they stop and bury some of the gold so they could make better time. He pointed out that they could live in style in Mexico with even half the gold. But at any talk of leaving gold behind Ford turned ugly.

Jim was unused to riding bareback and he felt the insides of his thighs begin to chafe. He shifted his seat, in the hope of finding a more comfortable position. Ford turned and asked, "Butt gettin' tired, kid?"

"For two cents I'd throw this gold in a ditch and ride for the border as fast as I could go."

"*Mayheeco* ain't a place to be poor in."

"Poor and alive is better'n rich and dead."

"They ain't caught us yet. They ain't about to."

"Wish I was only half as sure as you," Jim said. He shifted the lead ropes to his left hand to relieve the ache in his right arm. They didn't allow any of the animals to run loose, not even the burro. Their horse with its double weight wouldn't be able to run down the animals should one or all of them decide to go off on their own.

Regularly, Jim turned his head to study the trail behind them and was heartened to see no sign of riders. At least they'd managed to get this far undetected.

Jim scowled at the terrain which was blinding white under the sun. They were riding down a long, wide canyon. "How far to the border, now?"

"See that hump of mountain over east?" Ford inclined his head.

"What about it?"

"From what I heard in Grayfork, that's where Wheeler Springs is. From Wheeler Springs it ain't more'n a handful of miles to the line. Tell your belly to stop rumbling. Once we're in ol *Mayheeco* I'll buy you the best meal a man ever ate."

"Now is when I'd like that best meal."

Ford sniffed the air. "I can almost smell the border, it's that close."

"Don't smell different to me."

"You'll see." Over the hours, Ford seemed to have regained more of his strength, but at times his speech rambled and his laugh had an edge to it. "It'll be a fine time for us both, kid, when we split up that gold."

"The gold don't mean a damn to me, Ford."

"Stop moonin' about that gal. She was bony an' her eyes was too big for her head. Wait'll you see them black-haired ones across the line."

Jim was too tired to argue. He wondered just how Ford would know when they crossed into Mexico. All Jim could see on all sides of them were cactus-studded sand, arroyos, damn little shade, and no water. He could hear only a faint splash of liquid in the canteen tied to the saddle horn. He looked hopefully at a layer of dark clouds which was beginning to cover the blue sky. Would they bring rain? In this parched country had it *ever* rained? His mouth felt as if he had swallowed a half ton of dust and his stomach had never been emptier.

Ford was rambling on about some girl he had known in Nacadoches but Jim was too busy with the pack animals to pay much attention.

Suddenly Ford swore and yanked hard on the reins, causing the overburdened mount to swerve and nearly unseat Jim.

"Ford, what in hell's the matter?" Jim demanded.

"Somethin' moved up ahead!" Jim leaned over and peered beyond Ford's sweat-slicked neck. "Dead ahead," Ford said. "In them big rocks. You see anything?"

Jim froze. "Yeah." Two hundred yards ahead he made out the figure of a man half-concealed by a large boulder. The man was waving his hat in a signal to someone up on the rim of the canyon.

Chapter 17

Harper and Trent spent their first night in the hills surrounding Grayfork without sighting the Norcross brothers or finding their sign after they lost the trail where it ran into a full-flowing creek. Harper and Trent split up, Trent keeping to the east bank, Harper ranging far into the hills on the west side of the creek. But they were unable to find the spot the two had left the water, nor did they sight the brothers themselves.

They were hampered by the fact there was no moon, but Harper was not too concerned. It helped keep the fugitives out of the hands of the dozen riders who had gone pounding out of Grayfork to capture the pair that had shot up the town and stolen a horse, he reasoned. "Those hombres ever get it into their heads we're after a fortune in gold," Harper said grimly, referring to the posse, "we'd have a hell of a time gettin' that money home to Texas."

"A powerful lot of money," Trent said, avoiding

Harper's eyes. Changing the subject, he said, "Jim an' Ford sure didn't sprout wings. How'd they ever get away from us?"

"You got to learn patience, Bascom." Harper smiled as they stopped to rest their horses.

"While I learn patience, them two will be halfway to Canada with the money."

"Don't let them headin' north fool you none. Come daylight, we'll pick up their sign." They had ridden some miles up the creek into the higher hills. "I gotta hunch they didn't come this far."

"It better be a good one. Sometimes I think I can hear Arne Killebrew shoutin' all the way from Texas about that money we never brought home."

"Arne can be a mean son of a bitch when he wants to."

"You think I don't know that?" Trent sneered, the long chase beginning to wear down his disposition.

"You're just damn lucky that girl decided to get married or one of you Don Juans would be findin' it hard to fork a horse. Ol' man Killebrew'd take a knife to anyone who got his daughter in trouble."

Trent shifted in the saddle uncomfortably.

"So what d'you think Ford an' Jim are gonna do?"

"Ford is about as hard-nosed as Arne Killebrew. But Jim ain't like Ford, especially where gals are concerned. He might want to see that Delaney gal again."

"That's your hunch?"

Harper nodded. "According to what I hear, the Delaney ranch is on the way to the border."

"Makes sense to me."

"Let's hope that damn posse don't think of it. We don't want company when we run them two down."

"No, we sure don't," Trent agreed.

They grabbed a couple of hours sleep and then had jerky and cold biscuits for breakfast. Harper was in no hurry as they started down out of the high hills. He knew they could travel faster that the wounded Ford. He didn't know how badly Ford had been hit, but the impact had tipped him in the saddle, so it was more than a scratch.

By midmorning they picked up the tracks of two horses. It might have been cowhands or drifters, but Harper was sure it was the men they were following. And beside a dry camp, Harper found a piece of bloodied underwear that evidently had been used as bandage.

"Let's get after them," Trent said, ready to gallop off along the fresh set of tracks.

Harper shook his head. "We don't want to raise dust. No use letting Ford an' Jim know we're on their trail. And we don't want to bring down the posse on us either."

They found Delaney in his house with a bandage on his gashed head. His daughter was weeping bitterly.

Harper said, "We'll get 'em, Delaney. Which way'd they go?"

"I saw 'em head south. They had pack horses and a burro."

Harper felt a muscle twitch in his cheek. "That so? Wonder what they're carryin'."

"Would have gone after 'em," Delaney said, "but I was some dizzy after the young'un hit me over the head with his gun."

The girl, standing behind her father's chair, said brokenly, "I just can't understand how Jim could do that to my father. And all the other things they say he's done. It's—it's terrible."

"Miss, I feel sorry for how Jim tricked you all. But you'd best try to forget him. Him an' Ford is as good as dead already."

Delaney touched his bandaged head. "I'd sure like to ride with you boys. I'm feeling okay now."

"This is between us an' the Norcross brothers," Harper said. "We got five more men waitin' at Wheeler Springs. The Norcross brothers are as good as caught."

Ella Mae covered her face with her hands and left the room.

"My gal's takin' it mighty hard," Delaney said. "It ain't easy for a gal in country like this. Ain't often a young fella. . . . Damn his eyes! I trusted Jim. I never liked the other one they claim is his brother. But I did like Jim."

"Lucky you found out about him. Mebby Jim wasn't so bad by nature, but his brother's turned him into a real hell-raiser."

"You boys want fresh hosses?"

Harper said, "We won't be back this way, Delaney. These hosses we're ridin' belong to the 77 ranch in Texas an' we aim to ride 'em all the way home."

"You figure to take the Norcross boys back to Texas?"

Harper and Trent exchanged glances. Harper said, "We ain't likely to take Ford alive. Jim might give up. But then you never know."

"What'll happen to Jim if you do take him back?"

'My boss will see that he gets so many years in prison it'll give a man a headache just to tally 'em up."

A few hours later they were far to the south, crossing a range of mountains. The air smelled of dust and dark clouds were rolling in over the deep canyon they were riding along.

Trent said, "Jeez, a gully-washer will blot out their sign." They had picked up the trail of the fugitives seven miles back, at the entrance to a long canyon that twisted south.

"Rain or not, we'll catch 'em this time," Harper said. He leaned forward in the saddle and then pointed. "There they are."

Far down the canyon Trent spied two moving specks momentarily visible against a sheer cliff of pale rock. As the two men reined in to study their quarry the specks blended in with the rough terrain and were lost.

"You sure it ain't Apaches?" Trent said. "I'm partial to my scalp."

"We'll cut ahead. You take one side of the canyon, up on the ridge. I'll take the other." Harper gestured at a rock formation at the end of the canyon some miles ahead. "We'll meet there."

"You sure it's them?"

"I'll bet my life on it."

"We could ride 'em down right now and get it over with."

"They'd likely hear us comin'. Ford would hole up in the rocks and try an' pick us off."

"He's in no condition to stand us off long."

"He's still in the saddle and that means he can shoot. Ford's got more guts than ten men."

"I don't know about that."

"He stole the money. With odds eight to two. An' you really couldn't count Jim 'cause he was scared white. No, if you want the truth, Ford done it all by himself."

Trent chewed on this a while, then said, "We could sure as hell keep 'em holed up till the rest of the boys come up from Wheeler Springs."

Harper checked his rifle, then slammed it back into the boot. "Let's you an' me do it alone, Bascom."

Their gazes locked, then Trent nodded his assent

and started off along the right side of the canyon. He cut through a long groove in the canyon wall, climbing toward the ridge. He hoped to hell the going would be easy up here. He'd been in the saddle chasing the elusive Norcross brothers so long that he felt rooted to it. From higher ground he looked back down the slope and saw Harper heading along the opposite side of the canyon. Now what do you suppose Cale Harper meant exactly by *"Let's you an' me do it alone,"* Trent wondered.

Chapter 18

Jim could see the man plainly. It was Bascom Trent; he was sure of it because of the man's size. And now they could see another rider cutting in from the opposite side of the canyon. Cale Harper.

"They got us cut off," Jim said in a tight voice.

Ford stood up in the stirrups painfully. "I had a feelin' there was somebody watchin' us from up yonder." He nodded to the ridge. "Saw a puff of dust a time or two."

"What'll we do now?" Jim asked.

"About two miles back we passed a slot in the canyon that looked clear to me. I had a hunch to take it then. We'll take it now. They'll have a damn long wait for us down yonder." Ford's laughter was shaky.

"Ford, they'll run us down."

"Not if we get goin'." Ford turned the horse and with Jim tugging at the pack horses and the burro headed back up the canyon. A hawk floated on air currents far above them and seemed to jeer at their antlike progress. Before they retraced their steps a quarter of a mile the clouds thickened and the wind began to blow dust into their faces. The stolen Morgan horse did not like the load on its back nor the weather. It snorted and shook its head from side to side. Jim yanked it along with the other pack horse and the burro.

"Let's hole up in the rocks," Jim pleaded.

"We'll keep movin'," Ford said stubbornly.

"What if the others are waiting for us up ahead?"

"We'll unlimber them shotguns, little brother."

Jim licked his dry lips. What would happen when Ford realized the weapons had been left behind? "I don't want to kill anybody."

Ford laughed, then clutched his side with a groan. "Kill them or they kill us," he said.

"All this misery just for a little gold."

"A *little* gold?"

Jim felt a drop of rain on his cheek. "Maybe the rain will wash out our tracks and we'll be able to get away" he said hopefully.

But before long even Ford seemed to realize their pace was much too slow. "All right, kid." He nodded toward a circle of rocks to the left of the canyon. "Somebody made a stand there. So will we." In the center of what appeared to be a natural rock fortress were the remains of a partly burned freight wagon.

Jim stared around Ford's shoulder at the burned wagon. "Don't look like they did so good."

"We'll do better."

In the rock enclosure Jim slipped down from the horse's rump. Quickly he wrapped lead ropes of the three pack animals around a stump of cholla. Beyond a wagon wheel lying half-buried in the sand he saw a skeleton with a piece of leather shirt left on its ribs and nearby the remains of a boot.

Jim shivered. Not a very lucky place to make a stand. He slipped his rifle from the pack. Far down canyon they saw the twin riders approaching.

Ford leaned against a rock and watched them. His breathing was ragged, Jim noticed, and his face, what Jim could see of it, looked awfully pale. It was sheer nerve that had kept his brother in the saddle all these hours.

Ford turned his head; his eyes were glassy with fever. "Get out the shotguns and load 'em. When them bastards get close we'll cut 'em to pieces."

"Ford, we forgot the shotguns. They're back where we buried the gold."

Ford stared, trying to comprehend. "You forgot them? What kind of a stupid damn bastard son of a bitch are you?" Ford raged. Then he calmed down. "All right, we'll use rifles. Let 'em get close an' don't try for a head shot. Aim for the chest or guts. Then you'll be sure not to miss. I learned that in the war, kid."

"I'm not sure I want to shoot anyone, Ford."

"Oughta be easy for you to kill Bascom Trent. After the way you an' him fought over that no good Nadine Killebrew."

Rain began to pelt down. A lot of good it would do them now with the enemy not two hundred yards down the canyon.

"Why don't we give up, Ford? We'll never get away."

"Christ, kid, are you loco? They'd kill us without thinkin' twice. Now get ready. They'll be in range directly."

Jim stared down the canyon through the slanting rain. There was only one rider now—Cale Harper.

Jim peered frantically through the downpour, hearing it pound against his hat. *Where was Trent?*

Ford also missed the big man. He got to his feet and peered over the rock wall. "Where'd he go?" Ford looked to his right beyond Jim. "Where's that goddam Bascom?"

Jim saw his brother's head jerk, then Ford collapsed as a rifle shot cracked from the east side of the canyon.

"*Ford!*" Jim rushed to his brother's side. Kneeling in the wet sand he touched Ford's head, then saw the neat hole in his temple. Dark blood was dripping down onto the sand.

As Jim crouched there another bullet ricocheted off the rocks. The Morgan horse pitched over, spilling the gold across the rain-soaked sand. Panicked now, Jim sprang for the saddle. Another shot zinged by, sending up a geyser of sand. Jim spurred the roan into a dead run toward the north end of the canyon, away from the pair who sought to cut him off from the south and east. As he passed through the sheltering of rocks, Jim turned in the saddle to look back at Ford lying there on the sand with the sacks of spilled gold all around him.

Jim crouched low in the saddle, making himself as small a target as possible. Rifles spoke behind him but he could barely hear them above the roaring desert storm. In that instant of flight he thought of those in the past who had undoubtedly suffered from lack of water in this canyon and even died of thirst. In the narrowing parts of the canyon the water was beginning to run inches deep. Then, as quickly as it had come, the rain tapered off. Already Jim could feel the heat burning through the thinning cloud cover.

Ford, you've got your gold now. Jim wanted to

weep for his brother, but where the hurt should be was only an empty feeling. His horse faltered and he slowed the animal to look around him at the dazzling slope of wet rock. Where to hide?

Chapter 19

Harper dismounted and shook the water off his hat brim. He stared down at Ford. "The loco son of a bitch," the 77 foreman said tiredly.

Bascom Trent said, "Crazy, but rich." He looked at the octagonal coins that had spilled from the pack of the dead horse. The big Texan gave a long whistle and met Harper's eyes. They looked at each other for a full half minute as the rainstorm moved on and the ground began to steam under the strong sun.

Harper stepped across Ford's body and went over to where the burro and the other pack horse were tied. He ran a hand over the leather sacks the animals carried.

"Looks like it's all here, Bascom." Harper's voice betrayed a strain. "We had about this number of sacks at Abilene. Countin' the busted ones on the ground."

"Yeah, Cale. Reckon Arne Killebrew won't hang us to a barn rafter now. If we get that *dinero* back to him."

Their eyes met again. Harper turned to look south where a breeze was parting the clouds to reveal a patch of startlingly blue sky. "Down there is Mexico."

Trent nodded, his wide face betraying no emotion. "Mexico," he echoed.

"We're a lot closer to the border," Harper mused, turning back to look at the spilled coins on the sand, "than we are to Texas."

Trent was also staring at the coins. "Texas is a far piece from here, Cale."

"It'd take you an' me an' ten other hombres a dozen lifetimes to earn this much money." Harper said.

Trent was reloading his rifle. "Let's go after Jim an' finish him." He paused. "Then we'll come back for the gold."

Harper gave the Texan a hard grin. "When we started out for Kansas I figured to make your life miserable as hell. An' here we are partners."

"Thanks to that crazy bastard." Trent gestured with his rifle at Ford.

Just as the two men turned for their horses, they heard hoofbeats. Harper swore and peered to the south in the direction of the sounds. "Nobody's goin' to steal this gold," he muttered, cocking his rifle. Then he recognized the oncoming riders—the shirt-tail ranchers Sandy Burkhardt and Doc Thorne and the 77 hands Jennings, Reivers, and Cass.

"We heard the shootin'," Thorne cried as he spurred up. He swung down. "The gold here?"

"Looks like all of it, Doc." Harper's eyes met Trent's briefly, then slid away. Thorne was eagerly gathering up the spilled coins.

"Thank God," he said. "Thank God. Without my share of this pool money, I'd have been busted flat."

"Me too," said Burkhardt. He dismounted stiffly

and walked over to stare down at Ford Norcross in the sand. "He almost beat us, didn't he boys?"

"Did you get Jim?" asked Jennings, looking around.

Trent answered. "Was just figuring to go after him."

Harper realized suddenly that he was gripping his rifle unusually hard, his finger tight against the trigger. He slowly relaxed and his hold on his rifle loosened. For the first time he realized what could motivate a man like Ford to take such enormous risks. Never before had Harper been tempted to steal. Given the right set of circumstances, he now saw, there is a little thief in every man.

When he turned his head he saw Trent looking at him, a crooked smile on his lips. And Harper knew that the same thoughts had been going through Trent's head.

Harper made a little shrug of resignation, then turned to the others. "Sandy, you an' Doc stay with the gold. The rest of us will ride Jim down."

Jennings had noticed the half-buried skeleton near the charred wagon. "Who you s'pose he was?"

"Another unlucky hombre. Like Ford Norcross." Harper pulled his hat brim low. It had started to rain again. "I bet it ain't once in ten years they get a storm like this."

Trent pointed at the tracks left by Jim's horse. "We better get a move on or them tracks will be washed out."

They mounted up and moved out. Harper raised his voice above the sound of the driving rain, "What'll we do with Jim when we catch him?"

"Nothin' to do but kill him." Trent seemed surprised. "Thought we already decided that."

Tom Cass said, "It's a far piece to ride him back to Texas, but I reckon we should."

"Why?" demanded Harper.

"Jim can tell Killebrew what happened an' why we're so late gettin' home with the money."

"Arne won't give a damn about Jim's explanation," said Harper. "All he wants is the money."

The tracks of Jim's horse led up a lateral canyon. They knew it was only a matter of half a mile or so before they closed in on him.

Harper saw him first, far ahead, almost lost in the rain. Jim was moving slowly. Harper drew his rifle. "There ain't a tree around here to hang him to. So . . ." He halted his horse and through the rain drew a bead on the slim figure of Jim Norcross, outlaw.

Chapter 20

A kind of numbness had replaced Jim's shock at losing his brother. It was the same numbness he felt whenever he thought of Ella Mae Delaney. He was resigned to the inevitable. For the last quarter hour he had sensed the men pursuing him, then he had actually seen them, back in the rain where the trail began its climb through the canyon slot. His horse was about done in. He leaned over and patted the animal on the neck.

"You been through hell," he said. "So have I."

The horse stumbled, its forelegs collapsing. Just as this happened a shot slapped into the animal's hip. Jim could feel the shock of it run through the horse as it plunged headfirst into the rocks. Jim barely had time to kick free of the stirrups. As he was falling he managed to double up and roll.

At the bottom of the slope Jim bounded to his feet, hand to his revolver so as not to lose it. He began to run blindly up through a notch in the sandstone wall where water rushed down the normally parched gutter of stone and sand. His fingers bled as he dug into rock crevices seeking handholds.

He reached the crest and keeping low, looked back. He could see them in their yellow slickers gathered around the dead horse. They were talking and one—he thought it was Harper—shook his head.

Jim didn't know it but Harper was saying, "The border's close by. I don't figure to chase him into Mexico. We got the gold and that's what we come for."

They started riding back the way they had come, into the driving rain, and were soon lost to sight.

A week later, Jim was hobbling along on blistered feet. He looked up and saw a Mexican approaching on a wiry pony. Jim leaned against a boulder, breathing hard. He had the feeling that he had been wandering in circles for days.

He tried to remember some Spanish. *"Dónde está . . ."* His mind, fuzzed from fatigue, refused to respond. "Where am I?" he said in English.

The Mexican answered, "You are in Mexico, Señor. The border is ten miles to the north."

Jim looked around at the sand and cacti. It was not the verdant paradise his late brother had promised. Where were the creeks running full, the green hills?

"Hell, it's no different than Arizona," Jim said in dismay.

The Mexican shook his head sadly and started to ride on.

Jim thought back on the weeks of terror he had endured, alleviated only by the few happy days he had spent with Ella Mae. Now Ford was dead and the gold was back in the hands of its rightful owners. They had risked their necks twenty-four hours a day and for what?

Jim looked north. Up there, less than a dozen miles away, was the U.S.A. He knew he could never go back. In his brief career as outlaw he had killed only one man, a rustler, and he had spent none of the gold he had helped to steal. But even so he was a fugitive.

Well, he would have to make his life here in Mexico from now on. What else was there to do? He called after the Mexican, "Señor, Señor . . ."

At first he thought the man was going to ride off, fearful that Jim would try to rob him. But he must have decided the *norteamericano* was harmless. He halted his horse and turned in the saddle to wait for Jim to catch up.

"Where is the nearest village?" This time Jim's Spanish came out all right and the Mexican understood. He pointed a gloved hand toward the south. Then he said, "You work cattle?"

Jim nodded. "It's all I know how to do. And I'm good at it."

"In the village ask for Rodolfo Gomez. He will pay fifteen dollars a month American money to a man who knows cattle."

"Fifteen dollars a *month*?"

"It is all you can expect. Down here we are poor."

Jim shook his head helplessly. Would he ever learn the extent of Ford's deception? Green trees, gold, and *ricos*.

"You have a name?" the Mexican asked softly.

"Ford. Jim Ford," said Jim. He reckoned it was the least he could do for his dead brother. He would carry his name into the barren land he had dreamed about for so long.